Springtime for Henry

A Farce in Three Acts

by Benn W. Levy

A SAMUEL FRENCH ACTING EDITION

SAMUEL FRENCH

FOUNDED 1830

New York Hollywood London Toronto

SAMUELFRENCH.COM

The play was first publicly performed on December 9th, 1931, at the BIJOU THEATRE, *New York, with the following cast:*

Mr. Dewlip	LESLIE BANKS
Mr. Jelliwell	NIGEL BRUCE
Mrs. Jelliwell	FRIEDA INESCORT
Miss Smith	HELEN CHANDLER

CHARACTERS IN THE PLAY

(in the order of their first appearance)

MR. DEWLIP

MR. JELLIWELL

MRS. JELLIWELL

MISS SMITH

The action of the play takes place in the
sitting-room of MR. DEWLIP's flat.

ACT ONE

*An extremely untidy room with two doors. It shows signs
of a comfortable, wealthy owner but one not particularly
house-proud. A very grand gramophone is noticeable, with
a roulette wheel leaning haphazard against it. There are
drinks available from a collapsible cabinet.*

*The central door [the one leading to the small front hall]
is banged violently. Some one has left in a temper. Almost
simultaneously from the door on the right leaps* MR. DEWLIP.
MR. DEWLIP *is also in a temper. He hurls after his late visitor
a large handful of papers that he is carrying, but they
flutter harmlessly against the banged door and fall to the
ground like snow in a nightmare.* MR. DEWLIP, *a well-fed,
well-groomed man a year or two under forty, grinds his
teeth. He paces in rage. He picks up a tumbler, and sends
it hurtling into the fireplace. He kicks a chair off its
balance. He is about to kick a heavy desk but recalls himself in time to drop a cushion as shock-absorber between
desk and toe. On some of the papers scattered on the
ground he deliberately wipes his feet. His eyes fall on a
telephone directory and he searches for a number with a
violence that leaves the book in tatters.* MR. DEWLIP, *in
short, is in a rage.*

DEWLIP. [*at the telephone*] Regent 2403. . . . Yes. . . .
[*While he waits, he seizes a cigarette, but, finding he has*

3

no matches within reach, chews it nervously. Soon his mouth is unpleasantly full of tobacco-ends, which he spits forth angrily] What? . . . No, I didn't say anything. . . . Is that Regent 2403? This is Mr. Dewlip, Mr. Henry Dewlip. . . . I'm in a rage. . . . What? I say I'm in a rage. . . . Yes, my girl has just left me. The one you gave me. She bounced out of the place about two minutes ago. . . . No, bounced. . . . What? No, I was not rude to her. She called me names. . . . No, I didn't say a word about her. I said something about her mother but not a word about her. Then out she bounced. . . . No, bounced. . . . Yes, of course I want another girl and it *is* urgent. . . . No, I would not have the same one back. She was no good anyway. Besides she snored dreadfully and I never got a wink of sleep. . . . Well, let's come to the point. . . . Well, what have you got? . . . Yes? . . . Yes? . . . Efficient? . . . All right, send her along as soon as you can. [*He replaces the receiver, lights a cigarette and, his temper improved, sets the gramophone playing. While he is sitting beside it, rather on the edge of his chair, the center door opens and* MR. JELLIWELL *comes in; a large, self-assured, humorless man of about the same age as* DEW-LIP, *rather like the conventional idea of an Anglo-Indian, though he is not one.*]

JELLIWELL. Morning, Henry.

DEWLIP. Hello, Johnny. Where did you spring from?

JELLIWELL. I was just passing; thought I'd look in. Rather wanted to have a word with you. What are you doing there?

DEWLIP. Playing the gramophone. I play it rather well.

JELLIWELL. But why are you sitting down to it?

DEWLIP. Is one supposed to stand up when playing the gramophone?

JELLIWELL. No; I just thought you looked rather peculiar sitting there alone with nothing in your hands. [*vaguely*] I don't know what it was. It was just your sitting there somehow. What are you playing?

DEWLIP. [*getting up and stopping it*] Be careful!

JELLIWELL. [*starting*] What of?

DEWLIP. Those papers. Don't stand on them, you fool. Those are all extremely important papers.

JELLIWELL. What a damn silly place to keep them.

DEWLIP. I don't keep them there. They're just there—temporarily.

JELLIWELL. Why?

DEWLIP. I have my own reasons.

JELLIWELL. Do you often put your papers—er—down there?

DEWLIP. I didn't put them there. I—I threw them at a lady.

JELLIWELL. [*unsurprised*] Did you hit her?

DEWLIP. No, I missed her.

JELLIWELL. How many shots were you allowed?

DEWLIP. One, and no prizes. You find me this morning in an extremely evil temper.

JELLIWELL. Pity. You're usually rather cocky.

DEWLIP. [*severely*] I have a sunny disposition but I am never cocky.

JELLIWELL. Sorry. What's gone wrong?

DEWLIP. My secretary's just thrown me over: without any warning.

JELLIWELL. Thrown you over? I'd no idea you were going to marry her.

DEWLIP. I had no intention of marrying her. I never marry my secretaries. I merely meant she'd thrown up her job: suddenly without notice. And here I am left helpless. Besides, I'd got used to her. She'd been with me longer than any of her predecessors: three weeks next Friday.

JELLIWELL. What was it all about? Did you—

DEWLIP. No, I never laid a finger on her.

JELLIWELL. So she left? Got anybody else?

DEWLIP. Got anybody else! After half-an-hour! You can't get a secretary as you'd get a rasher of bacon.

JELLIWELL. I don't see why not.

DEWLIP. As a matter of fact I'm expecting one to come and see me, at any time now: somebody who lives in this building. They're ringing her up. By the way, how did you get in? I didn't hear the bell.

JELLIWELL. I didn't ring it. I found the front door open so I walked in.

DEWLIP. Careless little slut!

JELLIWELL. Who the devil are you talking about?

DEWLIP. Not you: my secretary.

JELLIWELL. Oh, *she* left it open, did she! If you ask me I should say she's bust it. I couldn't shut it after me. Slammed it, eh? Temper, temper, temper.

DEWLIP. I suppose I'd better send for a locksmith. Whenever a secretary leaves me, I have to send for a locksmith. Anyhow what did you want to talk to me about?

JELLIWELL. Well, perhaps it will do some other time, as you're in such a foul temper to-day.

DEWLIP. [*sourly*] I am in a particularly good temper.

JELLIWELL. Well, you ought to know. But it *did* just seem to me you weren't quite as cocky as usual.

DEWLIP. Will you kindly stop calling me cocky! I tell you I am in a particularly good and cheerful humor to-day and at peace with all the world! Now! Try and get that into your thick head.

JELLIWELL. All right, old boy, all right. No need to be abusive even if you are at peace with all the world.

DEWLIP. [*more quietly*] It's merely that I happened to have a particularly late night last night and haven't had a bite of luncheon to-day.

JELLIWELL. Why haven't you had any luncheon?

DEWLIP. Because I didn't want any luncheon.

JELLIWELL. Have any breakfast?

DEWLIP. I had a strong breakfast and soda at eleven, but nothing since. [*thoughtfully*] Perhaps that's what I need. [*He goes to the whisky.*] Drink for you?

JELLIWELL. Thanks: I wouldn't mind one. [DEWLIP *hands one to* JELLIWELL *and retains one.*] Your very good health, old boy. [*He drinks.*]

DEWLIP. [*complacently*] My very good health. [*He drinks, settling himself comfortably.*]

JELLIWELL. How did you come to be so late last night?

DEWLIP. [*jerking his head toward the roulette wheel*] Games of chance.

JELLIWELL. Oh, yes, I forgot. My wife was here.

DEWLIP. She was. Why don't you come next time?

JELLIWELL. Can't afford it, old boy. Nor could Julia for that matter, if she didn't always win.

DEWLIP. [*a little uncomfortably*] Julia's certainly very lucky. Anyway, that's not what you came to talk aboout. What was it?

JELLIWELL. Well, it's this. You've heard of Caribona Carburettors?

DEWLIP. I think so. Why?

JELLIWELL. Well, as a matter of fact, I *am* Caribona.

DEWLIP. The devil you are! Since when?

JELLIWELL. Since last Tuesday, to be exact. Me and one or two pals, we bought it up.

DEWLIP. My dear Johnny, you can't possibly say that.

JELLIWELL. Why not? It's true.

DEWLIP. It may be true, but it's not grammar. "Me and one or two pals bought it up!"

JELLIWELL. Well, what should it be?

DEWLIP. One or two pals and me bought it up.

JELLIWELL. Anyway, you knew what I meant.

DEWLIP. I did, but most people would not have known. Try and be a little more careful. Now go on.

JELLIWELL. Well, I *am* Caribona. That's the long and short of it. [*There is a silence.*] Go on, old boy, say something.

DEWLIP. I'll say anything you like, but what does one say when a man bursts in and announces "I am Caribona"?

JELLIWELL. Oh, you say, "Well done, old boy" or "Congratulations, old boy" or something.

DEWLIP. Well done, old boy.

JELLIWELL. Thanks, old boy.

DEWLIP. [*reflectively*] Caribona Carburettors. They're no good, are they?

JELLIWELL. Oh, they're not too bad. They just want a bit of ginger put into them.

DEWLIP. Ginger?

JELLIWELL. You know what I mean. The firm's been badly run; that's why we were able to get it comparatively cheap. The carburettors are all right: so we just said to ourselves, "All this show needs is a little ability and some ginger and guts and enterprise" and, if we've got any ginger and guts between us, we said, "by God we'll put them into it," we said.

DEWLIP. Well done, old boy.

JELLIWELL. And then I thought of you. "Here," I said to myself, "is a scheme by which we may both profit. What is the largest car-producing concern in Great Britain?" I said. "Dewlip Motors. Who is my oldest friend?" I said. "Henry Dewlip. What is the one complaint every one makes about Dewlip cars?" I then said. "Carburetion wonky."

DEWLIP. What's that?

JELLIWELL. Carburetion wonky, old boy.

DEWLIP. It's a lie; it's an ugly lie.

JELLIWELL. Oh no really; very wonky, I assure you. I've no reason to tell you wrong, have I?

DEWLIP. I don't believe you know a wonky carburettor when you see one.

JELLIWELL. Well, I ought to. After all I *am* Caribona.

DEWLIP. So I have gathered.

JELLIWELL. You see, wonkiness in a carburettor is a very tricky thing. Who makes your carburettors?

DEWLIP. I'm not sure. Draycott's, I think.

JELLIWELL. [*snorting contempt*] Draycott's!

DEWLIP. Well, what's the matter with Draycott's?

JELLIWELL. Oh nothing. Very good old-fashioned firm. You won't catch me running down a competitor. Ha! Draycott's! [*He affects a restrained laugh.*] Anyway, why not let us have a shot? Of course one doesn't want to be sentimental, but after all, I *was* at school with you.

DEWLIP. So was Draycott.

JELLIWELL. I was in the eleven with you.

DEWLIP. You ran me out. Besides Draycott was in the Lower Third with me.

JELLIWELL. So was I.

DEWLIP. Yes, and you used to pinch my behind during Algebra.

JELLIWELL. Oh no, old boy be fair. I only used to pinch your behind during Divinity. And after all, every one else used to, also. It was, if you will forgive my saying so, that kind of behind.

DEWLIP. I will not forgive your saying so. I consider the conversation is on the verge of becoming personal. Besides it isn't true. I shall not give Caribona Carburettors a trial.

JELLIWELL. Oh well, of course, if I'd known that after twenty years you were going to throw your rotten old behind up at me, I shouldn't have wasted my time.

DEWLIP. [*angrily*] Will you kindly allude to my person with proper respect!

JELLIWELL. Oh come now, my dear chap; don't let's quarrel about a silly little thing like that.

DEWLIP. [*still aggrieved*] Silly little thing like what?

JELLIWELL. I didn't mean to slight it. Honestly I wouldn't say a word against it. I don't know how it ever pushed its way into the conversation. After all, it's not a very nice thing to talk about.

DEWLIP. [*sulkily*] I don't agree. I think it's a very nice thing to talk about. Anyhow, now leave it alone.

JELLIWELL. Very well. I'd no idea you were sensitive about it. In any case I didn't come here to discuss—er . . . I came to discuss Caribona.

DEWLIP. And you have. I am very sorry not to be more helpful.

JELLIWELL. Is that your absolutely final decision? Won't you even let us send in a quotation?

DEWLIP. My dear Johnny, what's the use? You know I never interfere with the business.

JELLIWELL. You're chairman.

DEWLIP. That's only nominal. When my father died last

year, he left me the business just as he left me his watch and chain. And I never tinker with either.

JELLIWELL. But you could, if you wanted to.

DEWLIP. Of course I could.

JELLIWELL. Very well then?

DEWLIP. My father built up the best motoring business in England and was satisfied with Draycott's carburettors. Am I to change a thing like that with my father not yet cold in his grave? God knows I'm not a good man, but at least I wouldn't touch his carburettors till my father's at least cold in his grave.

JELLIWELL. I don't want to be indelicate, old boy, but don't you think, after nearly twelve months, he—er—*might* be cold now?

DEWLIP. You never knew my father.

JELLIWELL. No, I'm afraid not.

DEWLIP. Mind you, Johnny, I don't want you to think I wouldn't do anything I could to help you, but that is just the kind of thing in which I never interfere. By Jove, is that the right time? My dear fellow, you must go. What a nuisance! I'm expecting some one.

JELLIWELL. That's all right. Don't make any compliments with me.

DEWLIP. Right. I won't. Ring me up sometime and we'll have lunch. Good-by.

JELLIWELL. Good-by, old boy.

[*He goes.* DEWLIP, *who has rather anxiously sped the parting guest, makes an erratic and ineffectual attempt to tidy his room. He moves many things but achieves only a different untidiness. Eventually satisfied, however, he sets the gramophone a-playing and sits by it again on the edge of his chair. Presently a lady opens the door;* MRS. JELLIWELL. *She is five or six and twenty; dark, self-assured, elegant, extremely handsome, exquisitely gowned and groomed. He does not at first notice her; so she watches him for a moment, then, moving behind him, clasps her hands before his eyes.*]

JULIA. Who is it?

DEWLIP. [*ecstatically*] Beatrice!

JULIA. Pig! [*She moves from him.*]

DEWLIP. [*a little discomforted*] Julia! My mistake. That is an extremely silly trick of yours; a very silly trick. Numbers of happy lives have been wrecked by it.

JULIA. Rubbish. You were expecting me to tea. You knew perfectly well who it was. Didn't you?

DEWLIP. [*sulkily*] Yes.

JULIA. And you only said "Beatrice" in order to annoy me, didn't you?

DEWLIP. Yes.

JULIA. And there isn't a Beatrice, is there?

DEWLIP. I don't remember.

JULIA. And I want some tea.

DEWLIP. What kind?

JULIA. Martini. What exactly were you doing there?

DEWLIP. Playing the gramophone.

JULIA. But why were you sitting down to it?

DEWLIP. Is this a game?

JULIA Can't you answer a civil question? I merely said, why were you sitting down?

DEWLIP. Because I am in love.

JULIA. Do you always sit down when you're in love?

DEWLIP. No, I adopt a variety of positions but that is the one I favor most.

JULIA. Why?

DEWLIP. Oh, stop asking me questions!

JULIA. Then stop the gramophone. It has that effect on me. [*He does so.*] What about my drink? [*He goes to the cocktail cabinet, opens it, and proceeds to mix the drink. She lights a cigarette.*] You're very silent?

DEWLIP. I was thinking.

JULIA. What about?

DEWLIP. About last night. You said you wanted to see me on a private matter and I said that was strange as I also wanted to see you on a private matter. I was wondering if it could be the same private matter.

JULIA. I hardly think so.

DEWLIP. Then let's hear yours first.

JULIA. Have you ever heard of Caribona Carburettors?

[*He pauses in his shaking.*]

DEWLIP. I think so.

JULIA. Well, it's about Johnny.

DEWLIP. Johnny *is* Caribona.

JULIA. Exactly. How did you know?

DEWLIP. Johnny left here about ten minutes ago.

JULIA. He never told me he was coming.

DEWLIP. The call was not premeditated. It was an inspiration. With a little bad luck you might have met him on the stairs.

JULIA. I came up by the lift. What a narrow escape. Johnny's so absurdly suspicious. [*He hands her a cocktail.*] Thanks. Anyway, what did you decide?

DEWLIP. Decide?

JULIA. About Caribona. Did you give him the contract?

DEWLIP. No.

JULIA. Aren't you going to?

DEWLIP. No.

JULIA. But, Henry darling, you must! Why ever not?

DEWLIP. For a number of reasons. I explained them to Johnny.

JULIA. What were they?

DEWLIP. To begin with, my father's not quite cold in his grave.

JULIA. Rubbish. He's quite cold.

DEWLIP. Allow me to know best about my own father's— er—temperature.

JULIA. But I don't see what that's got to do with it.

DEWLIP. Naturally! You're a woman and aren't expected to understand business.

JULIA. But don't you realize that this contract is extremely important to Johnny—and to me? He had to borrow money to buy the business. We were counting on you.

DEWLIP. Confounded impertinence!

JULIA. I don't see why. I thought you liked me.

DEWLIP. I do like you. In fact I asked you here to-day with the express intention of making love to you.

JULIA. So I imagined. [*impudently*] It seemed to me the two things might possibly be connected.

DEWLIP. You were wrong. I dislike men who do business for love or women who make love for business. It generally means that they do both badly.

JULIA. Then why are you so punctilious in paying my losses at roulette?

DEWLIP. Purely a question of ingratiation. Women should be stolen and not bought.

JULIA. But I am not conscious that you have even stolen me.

DEWLIP. I was about to do so this afternoon.

JULIA. I wonder.

DEWLIP. You don't believe me?

JULIA. Your welcome was scarcely ardent.

DEWLIP. I have my own methods. As a matter of fact only this morning I wrote you a letter so willfully, so blazingly indiscreet that no woman could fail to be touched by it.

JULIA. I shall receive it to-night. How lovely!

DEWLIP. Er—well, perhaps not to-night. More probably in the morning.

JULIA. To sweeten my morning coffee!

DEWLIP. However, now that the Caribona question is disposed of, perhaps you would prefer to go.

JULIA. But I couldn't dream of going. You haven't even attempted to make love to me yet. *My* mission has failed; aren't you going to see if yours does?

DEWLIP. Very well. Have another cocktail first.

JULIA. Thank you. In case I need it. [*He refills their glasses and sits beside her.*]

DEWLIP. Will you drink to my mission?

JULIA. Yes, I think so. To your mission. [*They drink.*] Come along; begin.

DEWLIP. Right. Do you mind holding that in your other hand? [*She moves the glass into her right hand.*] Thanks. [*He takes her left in his and says a little prosaically.*] I want you.

JULIA. Thrilling!

DEWLIP. I want you—er—very much indeed.

JULIA. Exhilarating!

DEWLIP. What are we going to do about it?

JULIA. Oh, the poetry of those words!

DEWLIP. Don't be frivolous, Julia.

JULIA. Frivolous in the face of such a passion?

DEWLIP. My dear, we're not schoolchildren. I pay you the compliment of omitting the frills.

JULIA. Still I rather like the frills.

DEWLIP. [*with just a touch of impatience*] I've put them in my letter. For the moment let's keep to the point.

JULIA. I've rather forgotten what the point is.

DEWLIP. Then suppose you pay a little attention. I repeat: I want you.

JULIA. Yes, I distinctly recall your saying that.

DEWLIP. Now the next question is, do *you* want *me?*

JULIA. I'm glad that's to be considered too.

DEWLIP. Well, do you?

JULIA. I suppose you remember that Johnny is your best friend?

DEWLIP. I do, and I also remember that when we were in the Lower Third together, he used constantly—but supposing you answer my question.

JULIA. Won't you repeat it?

DEWLIP. Do *you* want *me?* [*She regards him for a second, her head tilted to one side.*]

JULIA. Yes. [*He beams at her, delighted. Then he finishes his cocktail.*]

DEWLIP. Now I'm going to kiss you.

JULIA. It's taken you long enough. [*He takes her in his arms and kisses her at great length.*]

DEWLIP. [*at last*] That was marvelous. Wasn't it?

JULIA. Yes.

DEWLIP. Happy?

JULIA. Yes; though it worries me when I think of Johnny.

DEWLIP. Johnny's a dear good fellow. Poor Johnny! [*He kisses her again.*]

JULIA. Wouldn't it be dreadful if he walked in and found me here!

DEWLIP. I don't see why. It's the middle of the afternoon.

JULIA. You don't know Johnny as I do. He's got a strong Puritan strain in him. Besides he adores me.

DEWLIP. I suppose we ought to tell Johnny. I couldn't stand a hole-in-the-corner intrigue: it needs too much energy.

JULIA. Do you want to marry me?

DEWLIP. [*clearing his throat*] Well—that raises rather an interesting point.

JULIA. Not uninteresting.

DEWLIP. I'll have to tell you something that scarcely anybody knows; not even Johnny. To put it bluntly, I *am* married.

JULIA. No!

DEWLIP. I was two and twenty. It was in America. She used to live by Niagara Falls. I often think it was that that got on her nerves. I brought her over here and we were married quietly in Cumberland. For a year we were very happy; and then—and then—[*He taps his forehead significantly.*] All to pieces. [*To conceal his emotion he blows his nose.*] She became convinced that I was Durham Cathedral. You can't imagine how inconvenient that was.

JULIA. Poor Henry!

DEWLIP. Ever since of course she's had to remain in a— in a—[*But he can't go on.*]

JULIA. Don't you say it, darling! Just forget it.

DEWLIP. In a home. They're very kind to her. It's in Glamorganshire. I try not to talk about it or think about it. But I wanted you to understand why I couldn't marry you.

JULIA. I understand. I shan't breathe it to a soul.

DEWLIP. Does it make any difference?

JULIA. Darling: of course not.

DEWLIP. Now what about telling Johnny?

JULIA. I don't quite see why we should.

DEWLIP. Well I think he'd like to know.

JULIA. What do you mean?

DEWLIP. I mean it seems only friendly.

JULIA. Supposing he shoots you?

DEWLIP. If he did, I should never forgive him. Do you think he would?

JULIA. I think at the worst he may shoot you, at the best he may pull your nose.

DEWLIP. Is that the best?

JULIA. What would you do?

DEWLIP. I don't know. I should probably pinch his— Have another cocktail?

JULIA. No, thank you.

DEWLIP. Well, I will.

[*As he goes to serve himself*, JELLIWELL *bubbling over*

with joyous excitement bursts into the room. JULIA *gasps.*]

JELLIWELL. [*seeing* DEWLIP *only at first*] I say, Henry! The most marvelous adventure. Happened almost as soon as I left the building. [*Suddenly seeing* JULIA, *he greets her amiably.*] Hallo, Julia darling: fancy seeing you here. [*That is all: then he continues exuberantly, while the others remain speechless.*] Damn nearly run over, she was. Had to leap ten feet into the air to save her skin. Wasn't touched, as it happened, but it gave her the shock of her life. Here; where's the whisky?

DEWLIP. [*weakly*] Where's the whisky.

JELLIWELL. Thanks. Do you mind if I take it down to her?

DEWLIP. [*uncomprehending*] She's downstairs, is she?

JELLIWELL. Of course, old boy. She lives downstairs : two small rooms in the basement.

JULIA. Do you mind, Johnny, trying to explain what has happened?

JELLIWELL. I've told you, darling. She was very nearly run over. I was passing and of course asked if I could do anything. At first, to my surprise, she said no.

DEWLIP. Did you explain that you *were* Caribona?

JELLIWELL. Don't be damn stupid, old boy. She said she was quite all right, thank you : but she looked a bit green, so I walked alongside of her to the door. On the way she did just stagger a little once—

JULIA. She was probably intoxicated.

JELLIWELL. [*ignoring her*] A kind of delicious, graceful stumble. You know what I mean, like this. [*He demonstrates.*]

DEWLIP. Irresistible!

JELLIWELL. So I took her arm and brought her back to her room and laid her on her bed and opened her—er—opened her windows. And then I began hitting her in the face with a wet towel.

DEWLIP. Knotted?

JELLIWELL. Of course not, old boy. And then I just sat down and talked to her till the color came back to her cheeks.

JULIA. Which must surely have been instantaneous.

JELLIWELL. Anyway I must be getting back to her with the whisky.

JULIA. [*a little severely*] Just a moment, Johnny. Henry, I think you were right. We had better tell Johnny the news.

JELLIWELL. What news, darling?

JULIA. Henry will tell you.

DEWLIP. Perhaps really I should tell him alone.

JELLIWELL. What is it, old boy?

JULIA. It's about me, Johnny. I think I'll stay.

DEWLIP. Very well. Johnny, I have been seeing a great deal too much of your wife lately.

JELLIWELL. Well, it's no good blaming me. You didn't have to.

JULIA. Henry is not complaining that he's bored with me, darling.

JELLIWELL. I should think not. I happened to marry a damned amusing little woman, didn't I, old girl? A regular little comic in fact, eh? [*He pinches her cheek.*]

JULIA. Don't do that!

DEWLIP. Listen to me, Johnny. I like your wife. Do you understand that? I like her very much.

JELLIWELL. Of course you do, my dear chap. I like her myself. And *we've* been married the best part of ten years.

JULIA. Six.

JELLIWELL. Six, is it? Thought it was more. I say I really must get along with the whisky. That poor girl's waiting.

DEWLIP. Johnny, I intend to deceive you.

JELLIWELL. You intend to what?

DEWLIP. I intend to wreck your married life.

JELLIWELL. [*goodnaturedly*] You know, I don't know *what* you're driveling about, old boy.

DEWLIP. I intend to steal your wife.

JELLIWELL. Who steals my wife steals trash. Who said that?

JULIA. Nobody said that. And one day you may be sorry that *you* did.

JELLIWELL. Oh, don't take offense, darling. No harm meant. The fact is you both seem to be talking such nonsense, I don't know where I am. Anyhow I mustn't wait any longer: really, Henry. [*He makes to go.*]

DEWLIP. I will make one more effort. Johnny, I want your wife to come to me.

JELLIWELL. Well, I may be a fool, but I've not the least idea what you're talking about.

DEWLIP. It's perfectly simple. I want your wife.

JELLIWELL. But whatever for?

JULIA. [*with indignation*] Henry: kindly drive me home.

DEWLIP. Very well. [*He takes up his hat from a chair.*] Johnny, my friend; you may be Caribona but you're a damn fool.

[*They go.* JOHNNY *looks after them in goodhumored perplexity for a moment, then goes to the whisky. He fills a glass but on his way to the door changes his mind and drinks it. While he is filling a second glass,* MISS SMITH *appears at the door. She is simply dressed, young, fair and with a certain ingenuous beauty that discords prettily with her rather independent manner.*]

JELLIWELL. Hallo. I'm afraid I've been rather a long time.

MISS SMITH. It doesn't matter. I came up to find you: to tell you not to bother. I'm feeling quite all right now. Thank you for being so kind to me.

JELLIWELL. [*a little distracted by the beauty of her*] Oh not a bit. When a man sees a lady in the street suddenly leap ten feet into the air as though she'd been punctured, what else could he do? There's a certain code about these things, you know. Won't you sit down?

MISS SMITH. I ought really to be getting back. [*But she sits.*] Is your friend out?

JELLIWELL. He went out about two minutes ago. What about your drink?

MISS SMITH. Oh no, thank you. I don't drink.

JELLIWELL. But you said downstairs you'd like something.

MISS SMITH. That was when I was feeling unwell. I only take it as medicine.

JELLIWELL. Do you? [*He looks longingly at the glass in his hand, then sets it down resolutely.*] I don't care for it either. [*He sits beside her.*] I say, I hope we meet again sometime. My—er—my first impressions of people never mislead me.

MISS SMITH. Your first impressions of me were of a young woman leaping ten feet into the air as though she'd been punctured. I don't always do that, you know.

JELLIWELL. Ah, I didn't quite mean that. As soon as I saw you, the thought flashed across my mind—if that woman's run over, it would definitely be—in my opinion at least—a pity.

MISS SMITH. No man could say more: especially as I went green with terror.

JELLIWELL. Did you?

MISS SMITH. Didn't I?

JELLIWELL. If you did, then I only wish all women were green.

MISS SMITH. [*coolly*] Is that a rather lame joke or an elephantine compliment?

JELLIWELL. I say, what do you take me for? I never make jokes.

MISS SMITH. It must therefore have been an elephantine compliment.

JELLIWELL. [*rather on his dignity*] It was a compliment certainly.

MISS SMITH. [*softening*] I didn't really mean to snub you but I hate compliments—at least after so short an acquaintance.

JELLIWELL. [*responding eagerly*] Of course you do. [*then rather overdoing the part*] I was a cad.

MISS SMITH. No. It's forgotten.

JELLIWELL. I say, do you realize, I don't even know your name?

MISS SMITH. Miss Smith. [*He bursts out laughing.*]

JELLIWELL. Oh, that's good! Miss Smith indeed!

MISS SMITH. What are you laughing at?

JELLIWELL. Oh I say! Miss Smith! Now you ask me what *my* name is.

MISS SMITH. Well, what *is* your name?

JELLIWELL. Mr. Brown! [*another paroxysm*]

MISS SMITH. [*smiling a little*] Oh *now* I see! What a strange coincidence! But honestly I don't think it's as funny as all that.

JELLIWELL. Perhaps it's not really. You see, I happen to have a particularly keen sense of humor. I always think a sense of humor is so important, don't you?

MISS SMITH. [*skeptically*] I do indeed.

JELLIWELL. I say, we *are* going to see some more of each other, aren't we?

MISS SMITH. That rather depends.

JELLIWELL. On what?

MISS SMITH. On you. You see, if we *are* to meet again, I shall have to take you in hand.

JELLIWELL. Will you? I don't quite know what you mean but I'm sure I shall love it.

MISS SMITH. How can I explain? Perhaps I'm not quite like most of the girls you meet. I like the Decent Thing.

JELLIWELL. [*a little out of his depth*] What's that?

MISS SMITH. I like men to be decent.

JELLIWELL. Well, what is there particularly indecent about me?

MISS SMITH. Why did you tell me you didn't care for drink?

JELLIWELL. But I don't.

MISS SMITH. Yet when I came into this room, I watched you gobble up the whisky you had prepared for me.

JELLIWELL. Oh not "gobble" really, Miss Smith.

MISS SMITH. I withdraw the "gobble" but you lied to me all the same. Why?

JELLIWELL. I don't know. I just had the idea that you might prefer me—er—not to care for drink.

MISS SMITH. You were right. I abominate men who reek of whisky. But I don't like liars either.

JELLIWELL. Oh I say, Miss Smith!

MISS SMITH. Then there's your attitude towards women.

JELLIWELL. What's wrong with that?

MISS SMITH. Shall we say a little—over-eager?

JELLIWELL. [*indignantly*] No, we shall not!

MISS SMITH. Of course I'm only judging by your attitude towards me.

JELLIWELL. Is it my fault that you happened to strike me as an extremely attractive young woman—when I saw you first?

MISS SMITH. Exactly. That was all that mattered to you. You never stopped to consider my soul.

JELLIWELL. Your what?

MISS SMITH. [*quite firmly*] My soul.

JELLIWELL. If I *had* stopped to consider it, you'd probably be run over by now. So possibly should I.

MISS SMITH. Instead you proceeded to deluge me with a bucketful of stale, gross, conventional, unconvincing, secondhand compliments to my body.

JELLIWELL. I may be gross but I prefer not to discuss your body till our acquaintance is a little older. Besides they weren't stale and secondhand: every nice thing I said (which by the way I now regret) rose to my lips as spontaneously as—as a dewdrop opens to the—er—the morning dew.

MISS SMITH. [*more kindly*] Perhaps then all I resented was your apparent facility.

JELLIWELL. Well, up to date you've managed to accuse me in the course of three minutes of being a liar, a drunkard, and a libertine. Are there any other complaints?

MISS SMITH. Yes; just one.

JELLIWELL. Oh. What's that?

MISS SMITH. I think every one ought to do a job of work. I don't like men who have nothing to do but kick their heels at half-past four in the afternoon.

JELLIWELL. Well, there you happen to be wrong, Miss Clever.

MISS SMITH. I beg your pardon?

JELLIWELL. I said, "There you happen to be wrong, Miss —Smith!"

MISS SMITH. I'm glad.

JELLIWELL. I have a very important job of work. As a matter of fact, I *am*—never mind. I only came here this afternoon for business reasons.

MISS SMITH. I'm afraid you'll think I've been very outspoken. It's only because if I like any one, I want them so terribly to be—you know—decent.

JELLIWELL. [*softened at once*] Then you do like me?

MISS SMITH. I hardly know you but I think I may.

JELLIWELL. In spite of all my—failings?

MISS SMITH. Perhaps I was wrong: perhaps after all you haven't so many.

JELLIWELL. Oh you weren't: I've led a worthless life. [*piling it up*] I see it all now. I've been a bad man.

MISS SMITH. [*ever so winningly*] Don't you think that, if I helped you, you might start afresh, turn over a new leaf?

JELLIWELL. *Would* you help me? [*She nods.*] I think I might. By God, I'll try.

MISS SMITH. Then for a start, try to stop swearing.

JELLIWELL. Miss Smith, you're wonderful. Already I begin to feel a better man. I say, I can't go on calling you Miss Smith.

MISS SMITH. What would you like to call me?

JELLIWELL. I think I should like to call you Andromache.

MISS SMITH. Why?

JELLIWELL. Don't you know the story of Andromache?

MISS SMITH. No.

JELLIWELL. Are you quite *sure* you don't?

MISS SMITH. Quite sure.

JELLIWELL. Well, the story of—er—Perseus and Androm-ache was a little like *our* story. Andromache was about the fastest girl they—er—ever had in Greece: a runner, you understand. She used to run after golden apples. So one day—er—Euripides offered a prize of half a pound of golden apples for the girl who—er—got there first. Well off they all went, hammer and tongs, tooth and nail,—er— Hades for leather, with Andromache leading of course by a good four lengths, when she suddenly caught her toe in something and tripped—just as you did just now in the street. Now it happened that Perseus was flying by at that moment with his Golden Fleece—just as I was just now, so to speak—and said to himself "By Jove, that's a—er—a maiden and a half! Poor little devil, she's crashed!" And down he swoops and picks her up. But no sooner had he set her down, top-side up, than I'm blowed if Juno, who was always a bit of a cat, doesn't turn her into an oak-tree! And an extremely elderly oak-tree too. So of course they've called the place—er—Clytemnestra ever since.

MISS SMITH. What a divine story! I adore mythology.

JELLIWELL. Oh, wonderful people the Greeks.

MISS SMITH. Are you a keen classical scholar?

JELLIWELL. Oh not really, you know. Not now. Haven't had time since I left school. But things come back to one. One doesn't really forget. [*He becomes the suitor again.*] Anyway that's why I feel I must call you Andromache. May I—Andromache?

MISS SMITH. Yes—Perseus. [*Their eyes meet and remain held a moment. She speaks a little abruptly.*] Honestly I must be getting back. I'm expecting a telephone call. Besides it's dreadful settling in a strange man's flat like this.

JELLIWELL. Oh he wouldn't mind.

MISS SMITH. [*looking about her*] He's very untidy, your friend. What kind of a person is he?

JELLIWELL. Awful. You wouldn't like him. I don't care much for my friend myself. He has all the qualities that you dislike. He's disgustingly rich—

MISS SMITH. I don't dislike that. It's not his fault.

JELLIWELL. He never does a stroke of work.

MISS SMITH. What about Dewlip Motors?

JELLIWELL. Inherited. He never goes near it. Then he drinks, swears, makes dreadfully long speeches and—and is very untruthful.

MISS SMITH. Oh dear, what a pity!

JELLIWELL. Gambling is about the only thing he devotes any time and attention to. He has giant roulette or "chemmy" parties here two or three time a week. [*He nods towards the roulette wheel.*] And always loses. And as for women, no woman is really safe in the same county with him. Finally he has a vile temper and he—er—will answer back.

MISS SMITH. Perseus.

JELLIWELL. Yes?

MISS SMITH. I want to ask you something.

JELLIWELL. What's that?

MISS SMITH. Are you married? [*He looks at her gravely for a moment; then rises, crosses to the window and stands staring through it.*]

JELLIWELL. You've raised a subject that I think I'd rather not talk about.

MISS SMITH. Oh, I'm so sorry.

JELLIWELL. No, it was not your fault. You couldn't know that it's a little painful to me. [*proudly, bravely*] I *am* married.

MISS SMITH. I see.

JELLIWELL. My marriage has not been a very happy one. My wife [*speaking with some difficulty*] is a mental invalid.

MISS SMITH. Oh, how dreadful!

JELLIWELL. Of course I don't mean she's dangerous—at least, I'm quite capable of looking after myself. But you can perhaps imagine that my married life has not been all roses.

MISS SMITH. Poor Perseus!

JELLIWELL. Oh no: don't think I'm asking for pity. I expect every one has his little cross to bear. All the same the divorce laws of this country are devilish unfair.

MISS SMITH. [*going to him and taking his hand*] I think there's something rather fine about you. I'm sorry I brought the subject up. Good-by, Perseus.

JELLIWELL. Good-by, Andromache. Can I see you down?

MISS SMITH. No, thank you. I'll go alone.

JELLIWELL. And we'll meet again? You know, you promised to help me. When?

MISS SMITH. You may ring me up. I'm in the book. Till then, don't forget: the Decent Thing. [*Their hands grip tighter.*]

JELLIWELL. [*earnestly*] The Decent Thing.

[*And she is gone. For a moment he stares, beaming, after her before wandering idly about the room in bland preoccupation. He halts instinctively by the whisky, flicks the decanter with his finger-nail, turns resolutely away. The telephone bell rings. He takes off the receiver and says without listening.*]

JELLIWELL. Number engaged.

[*He replaces it and saunters to the gramophone. As he winds it up, DEWLIP comes in.*]

DEWLIP. [*sourly*] Hallo. You still here?

JELLIWELL. Just off as a matter of fact. You mustn't think I've got nothing to do but kick my heels at half-past four in the afternoon.

DEWLIP. Who said anything about kicking your heels or kicking your anything else?

JELLIWELL. [a little superior] I must be getting along. They'll be waiting for me down at the office.

DEWLIP. [still with a bad grace] Just a minute. Do you still want that contract?

JELLIWELL. [suddenly eager again] Of course, old boy. Why?

DEWLIP. Then you'd better send in an estimate. Write to Davidson. I'll tell him to give you the details.

JELLIWELL. [overjoyed] But, my dear old boy! Why have you changed your mind? Why didn't you say that an hour ago?

DEWLIP. If I told you, you wouldn't understand.

JELLIWELL. I might. You never know. Try me.

DEWLIP. Because I happen to believe that women shouldn't be bought.

JELLIWELL. Why not, old boy? [an impatient movement from DEWLIP] Besides I don't see what that's got to do with it?

DEWLIP. I didn't suppose you would. [The telephone bell rings. DEWLIP answers it.] Hallo. . . . Yes. . . . Yes, it is. Wait a moment, will you? [*to* JELLIWELL] If you're in a hurry, I may be some time.

JELLIWELL. All right. I'll get along. Jove, what a wonderful afternoon! I say, Henry, I'm most frightfully obliged to you.

DEWLIP. Not at all. Good-by.

JELLIWELL. Good-by.

DEWLIP. [*on the telephone*] What? . . . No, the line hasn't been engaged for nearly an hour. . . . Well they *shouldn't* have said so.

JELLIWELL. Tch, tch! The telephone service is a public scandal.

[*He goes.*]

DEWLIP. Yes. . . . Yes. . . . Efficient? . . . Won't come? . . . What do you mean "refuses point-blank"? Why? . . . Well *I'd* rather you *did* say. Kindly tell me what she said. . . . Yes, I *do* insist. . . . Yes. . . . Yes. . . . [*ominously*] Go on. . . . Go on. . . .

[MISS SMITH *comes in, unnoticed, and stands quietly waiting.*]

DEWLIP. Go on. . . . [*uttering with difficulty*] What damned impertinence! What—damned impertinence! I'd teach her to "object to me on personal grounds"! I'd give her personal grounds! If she dared to show her nose in here now, I'd damn well tweak it. . . . No, you certainly will *not* try some one else. Did you think it necessary to telephone expressly to tell me that a common, little, knock-kneed, pigeon-chested, ugly, simpering chit of a girl [*She draws herself up.*] had the impudence to comment upon my morals and habits? Good-by. [*He slams down the receiver, he hurls a cushion across the room, he searches on the desk for papers but, finding none, takes some from a drawer and deliberately sends them hurtling after the cushion. Then his eye lights on* MISS SMITH. *He addresses her aggressively.*] Who the devil are you?

MISS SMITH. [*coolly*] Miss Smith.

DEWLIP. Who's Miss Smith?

MISS SMITH. Perhaps I'm interrupting.

DEWLIP. Get off those papers: they're important.

MISS SMITH. [*moving aside*] Really. Why are they there?

DEWLIP. They fell there.

MISS SMITH. I see.

DEWLIP. Who are *you?*

MISS SMITH. [*still detached and self-possessed*] I understand you are wanting a secretary?

DEWLIP. I am.

MISS SMITH. I am a secretary.

[*He has been watching her with growing admiration.*]

DEWLIP. [*quietly; pleased and surprised*] The devil you are!

MISS SMITH. The Burlington Secretarial Bureau sent me.

DEWLIP. The devil they did!

[*He just stares at her, fascinated, silent.*]

MISS SMITH. What are you staring at?

DEWLIP. [*absently*] Staring at. What am I staring at? Let me see now: what am I staring at? Nothing: nothing at all.

MISS SMITH. Is that all you have to say?

DEWLIP. Yes, that's all.

MISS SMITH. Don't you want to know any particulars about me?

DEWLIP. [*with a feeble effort at concentration*] Oh yes, I want to know that. Let me see: how old are you?

MISS SMITH. [*a little surprised*] Twenty-four.

DEWLIP. [*with a touch of ecstasy*] Twenty-four! Wonderful! What do you weigh?

MISS SMITH. I don't think I heard you correctly.

DEWLIP. I mean what are your speeds?

MISS SMITH. Fifty and a hundred and thirty.

DEWLIP. A hundred and thirty! Delicious! Turn around.

MISS SMITH. Why?

DEWLIP. [*his eyes beaming and never leaving her face*] I don't know.

MISS SMITH. Do you want references?

DEWLIP. No. You're engaged.

MISS SMITH. When shall I begin work?

DEWLIP. Now.

MISS SMITH. Very well. [*She takes off her hat, adding casually:*] By the way, I'm not pigeon-chested. [*The fatuous complacency is suddenly washed from his face.*]

DEWLIP. [*slowly*] What's that?

MISS SMITH. Nor knock-kneed.

DEWLIP. Are you . . . [*But he can get no further.*]

MISS SMITH. I am. I'm the ugly little chit of a girl who had the impudence to comment unfavorably on your morals.

DEWLIP. Well, I'll be damned.

MISS SMITH. That was precisely my point.

DEWLIP. You're sacked.

MISS SMITH. [*putting on her hat again*] Very good. You owe me a week's wages.

DEWLIP. Do I indeed!

MISS SMITH. Have you forgotten already that you engaged me? Four pounds, I think it is. That's what the Bureau told me.

DEWLIP. You whistle for it!

MISS SMITH. I don't whistle.

DEWLIP. And I don't pay a week's wages for nothing.

MISS SMITH. Very well. Then I'll work for a week. [*She takes her hat off again.*]

DEWLIP. For heaven's sake stop taking that damned thing off and on. It's making me giddy.

MISS SMITH. [*seating herself calmly at the desk and reaching for a pencil*] Do you wish to dictate?

DEWLIP. So it was you who had the cheek to criticize my habits. Who the devil do you think you are, I'd like to know?

MISS SMITH. Miss Smith.

DEWLIP. And how, may I ask, do you come to know anything about me?

MISS SMITH. How? Mr. Henry Dewlip of Dewlip Motors is so well known.

DEWLIP. And may I also ask what exactly my conduct has to do with you?

MISS SMITH. Nothing except on general principles. I happen to be what you would probably call rather strait-laced.

DEWLIP. Oh do you! Well, you'll very soon come unlaced if you stay here a week. If one of us has to change, it won't be me.

MISS SMITH. And it certainly won't be I.

DEWLIP. [*ignoring the correction*] In that case I don't think you'll enjoy yourself here.

MISS SMITH. I don't expect to but I have my living to earn.

DEWLIP. Perhaps it may interest you to learn that my last five secretaries left me in tears.

MISS SMITH. Really? Do you cry a lot?

DEWLIP. It was them who cried.

MISS SMITH. Your grammar isn't very good, is it? Do you wish to dictate?

DEWLIP. My grammar is excellent and I do wish to dictate.

MISS SMITH. Have you a writing pad?

DEWLIP. You can take it down straight on to the machine. I shall not go fast.

MISS SMITH. Where is the machine?

DEWLIP. On the floor beside the desk.

MISS SMITH. It looks rather heavy. Will you kindly lift it for me? [*He is about to refuse but, reluctantly changing his mind, does what she asks.*] Thank you.

DEWLIP. Kindly take two carbons.

MISS SMITH. Very good. [*She sets her machine in readiness.*] I'm ready. [*He clears his throat, glances at her resentfully, takes a turn up the room; then, still scowling, proceeds in a crisp businesslike style.*]

DEWLIP. "May 23rd, 1932. Darling." [*He looks surreptitiously to see if she flinches but she doesn't.*]

MISS SMITH. [*prosaically*] "Darling." Yes?

DEWLIP. "Darling, I have so much . . . to say to you . . . but somehow when I am with you"— Is that too fast?

MISS SMITH. Not in the least, thank you. "When I am with you"?

DEWLIP. "I can't say it. That is why . . . I am writing, although I shall be seeing you so soon."

MISS SMITH. "You so soon."

DEWLIP. [*still very businesslike*] "When I am with you, the scent of you—no, the luscious scent of you . . ."

MISS SMITH. "Luscious scent of you"? [*Her placidity enrages him.*]

DEWLIP. "Seems to make me drunk."

MISS SMITH. "Drunk."

DEWLIP. Drunk. [*He ponders.*] Drunk. "How I long to feel . . . your dear body shivering in my arms" . . .

[*He looks to see if he has shocked her yet but alas, he has not.*]

MISS SMITH. "Body shivering in my arms."

DEWLIP. No, "quivering."

MISS SMITH. "Pulsing" is more usual.

DEWLIP. Very well: "pulsing." "Pulsing in my arms. When shall that be? Till then, all my love to you, Henry" . . . I want you to make—

MISS SMITH. Just a minute, please. I haven't quite finished. [*He waits impatiently while the machine clicks on.*] Yes?

DEWLIP. I want you to make three copies of that. Send one to Mrs. J. Jelliwell, one to Lady Crighton and one to Miss Janet Harlowe. You'll find their addresses in the telephone book.

MISS SMITH. [*quite unperturbed, noting down the names*] Very good. Will you sign them yourself or shall I sign them per pro?

DEWLIP. I shall sign them myself of course. They naturally imagine I do my own typing.

MISS SMITH. I see. And shall I mark the envelopes "Private" or "Confidential"?

DEWLIP. Certainly. What do you expect to mark them? O. H. M. S.? I want the one to Mrs. Jelliwell to catch the next post.

MISS SMITH. Very good. [*He takes a turn or two.*]

DEWLIP. [*aggressively*] I suppose I've shocked you?

MISS SMITH. Not in the least. I'm not a baby.

DEWLIP. I didn't suppose you were.

MISS SMITH. By the way, you haven't tweaked my nose yet. [*She begins to type the envelopes.*]

DEWLIP. There's plenty of time.

MISS SMITH. You're annoyed not to have shocked me, aren't you? I'm sorry I couldn't oblige. You see, I knew what to expect.

DEWLIP. In that case why did you so suddenly change your mind and apply for the job?

MISS SMITH. If a traveler in a beautiful country comes across a slum, an eyesore, a plague-spot, he may either pass it by and put it out of mind or stop and try to do something about it. The second course has always seemed to me the more admirable.

DEWLIP. Meaning that I—correspond to the plague-spot?

MISS SMITH. Which I'm afraid it was my first impulse to pass by.

DEWLIP. God, if you were a man, if you were a man!

MISS SMITH. I very much doubt if I should have got this job. You asked me a question, and I answered you. Will you answer a question of mine?

DEWLIP. What is it?

MISS SMITH. Why did you engage me without references, tests or anything?

DEWLIP. Why? Because—er—because I was in urgent need of a secretary. [*She smiles and shakes her head.*]

DEWLIP. Why precisely should that make you grin like— like a cat on hot bricks?

MISS SMITH. Because I don't think that was a very truthful answer.

DEWLIP. Why do *you* think I engaged you? [*She faces him boldly.*]

MISS SMITH. Because you thought I was pretty.

DEWLIP. On the contrary I thought you quite revoltingly plain.

MISS SMITH. Then I was misled. As a rule when men think me plain, they don't beam fatuously and become incoherent in their speech.

DEWLIP. I am an exception. Ugly women make me extremely incoherent.

MISS SMITH. [*still smiling*] I see. Have you any other letters?

DEWLIP. Yes, I have. To L. P. Davidson, Dewlip Motors, Clerkenwell. [*a little absent-minded*] "May 28th, 1932. Dear—dear Davidson." [*He picks up the three letters she has typed.*] I'll post these myself. . . . "Dear Davidson" . . . What exactly was it that the traveler thought he ought to do about the plague-spot? [*She turns from her machine and looks at him.*]

MISS SMITH. [*for the first time almost friendly*] Let's drop that metaphor. It was rude of me.

DEWLIP. It was very rude of you.

MISS SMITH. You see I get a little carried away. Perhaps I'm rather different from most girls. I'm so tremendously keen on the Decent Thing.

DEWLIP. Go on.

MISS SMITH. Well, you rather put my back up; at least what I'd heard of you. You know what I mean: your idleness and cynicism and—and the drink and gambling and bad temper and the silly lies and—and the women. You know what I mean?

DEWLIP. You are lucidity itself.

MISS SMITH. So I thought perhaps, if only some one helped you all that might be changed. You might manage to make a fresh start.

DEWLIP. To turn over a new leaf, in fact?

MISS SMITH. Exactly. Won't you try? Do you think I could help you? What do you say?

DEWLIP. This is what I say. I say you are an impertinent, meddlesome, interfering little hussy with a vile complexion and I pray heaven that never again will a vindictive Providence visit me with such another. There!

MISS SMITH. [*gazing back at him, smiling, unflinching*] You know, you don't believe the bit about my complexion.

DEWLIP. I do.

MISS SMITH. Oh no, you don't. That was just bad temper. Still you believe the rest. I'm not discouraged. Much can happen in a week. I shall make my effort.

DEWLIP. If I catch you doing anything of the kind, I shall carry out my promise and pull your nose.

MISS SMITH. Then why not pull it now? [*She pushes it up at him impudently.*]

DEWLIP. Is that a challenge?

MISS SMITH. It is. [*Slowly, deliberately he grasps her nose between his forefinger and thumb. She does not budge.*]

DEWLIP. Let me ask you finally, once and for all, do you intend to reform me or not? [*Nasally she answers something inaudible.*] What's that? [*She repeats it.*] I can't hear a word you say.

MISS SMITH. [*bellowing*] How do you expect be to bake byself heard with fourteed-stode straphanging od by dose?

DEWLIP. Fourteen stone indeed! Under twelve stone.

MISS SMITH. That's quite edough.

DEWLIP. Do you intend to reform me or not?

MISS SMITH. I bost certaidly do.

DEWLIP. Very well. [*Very gently he tweaks her nose. For a moment or two they face each other, he in the acutest discomfort, she on the verge of tears.*]

MISS SMITH. You're a beast.

DEWLIP. I'm not. You insisted.

MISS SMITH. [*trying not to cry*] Will you kindly apologize?

DEWLIP. [*trying to maintain his bold front*] No: I will not. Do you expect me to say I did it by mistake?

MISS SMITH. You're not a gentleman.

DEWLIP. Isn't it lucky? If I were, you'd have nothing to reform.

MISS SMITH. I think we'll go on with the letters. [*There is a catch in her voice and, as she sits in front of the machine, the tears begin to flow. The fact distresses* DEWLIP *beyond measure but he manages not to surrender.*]

DEWLIP. [*unhappily*] "May 28th, 1932. Dear Davidson."

[*A long pause while he eyes her shaking shoulders wretchedly. Soon his glance lights on the letters in his hand.*]—"Dear Davidson." [*Surreptitiously with his back turned to her, he tears the letters across, hiding the fragments in his pocket.*] "Dear Davidson."

CURTAIN

ACT TWO

ACT TWO

Nearly three months later. The room now presents one conspicuous contrast: it is tidy. It is about half-past six, and MISS SMITH *is busy clearing up her chattels, when* MR. DEWLIP *comes in. His face is a little grave, but then immediately clears and assumes the benign expression of an amiable curate.*

DEWLIP. Well, well, Miss Smith! Half-past six and you still here? You ought to be resting. I mustn't overwork you, you know. Let me help you tidy up.

MISS SMITH. [*no less amiable*] No, it's quite all right, thank you. I've practically finished. I delayed on purpose really. I did so want to know what's happened about your carburettors.

DEWLIP. How sweet of you to want to know!

MISS SMITH. I expect you've had a terribly tiring day at the office?

DEWLIP. Well, I *was* pretty busy. But there: I always say work does a man good. Kicking one's heels about idly is extremely damaging to the soul. Don't you agree?

MISS SMITH. Oh, I do.

DEWLIP. What I always say is, Satan finds work for idle hands. That's what I always say.

MISS SMITH. Do tell me about the carburettor. I'm so excited. Have you got all the details yet?

DEWLIP. We had them all before us this morning: estimates for installing our own plant, and everything. It really looks even rosier than I expected. According to conservative calculations we reckon that, by manufacturing ourselves carburettors of my design, we shall make an annual saving of over £9,000, and pay for the cost of installation inside five months.

MISS SMITH. Oh, how marvelous! Mr. Dewlip, you must be proud.

DEWLIP. Proud? Ah, pride is rather a dangerous thing, you know.

MISS SMITH. I think you're wonderfully modest. And your own invention, too!

DEWLIP. Hardly an invention: only a new design. Besides, I've always been fascinated by motors and mechanical things ever since I was a little tot. By George, I'm thirsty. [*He pours himself out and drinks a glass of iced water.*] Has Mr. Jelliwell rung up here by any chance? Not a word from him at the office.

MISS SMITH. He hasn't rung up here. Were you expecting a message?

DEWLIP. I can't understand it. It's nearly a week since I wrote canceling his contract, and I haven't had a line in acknowledgment.

MISS SMITH. Perhaps he's sulking.

DEWLIP. Perhaps I ought not to have canceled it. After all, he *was* in the Lower Third with me.

MISS SMITH. I don't see that at all. Dewlip Motors is not a philanthropic institution. If your own carburettors are better and cheaper, you certainly ought to use them.

DEWLIP. Well, that was how I argued.

MISS SMITH. Have you come straight from the office?

DEWLIP. [*with a forced lightness*] Straight from the office? No, as a matter of fact I called on Dr. Bannerman: nice chap, old Bannerman.

MISS SMITH [*concerned*] Weren't you well?

DEWLIP. Oh, not really bad, you know. It just happens that I haven't been feeling too fit sometimes lately. Periodical giddiness, and so on.

MISS SMITH. What did he say was the matter?

DEWLIP. He didn't know. He asked me to tell him. He's a doctor, you know.

MISS SMITH. And did you tell him?

DEWLIP. I told him it seemed to date from the moment I cut myself off from all alcohol.

MISS SMITH. What did he say?

DEWLIP. He said my heart might be a little affected as a result. He had known such cases. I should have dropped it gradually.

MISS SMITH. Disgusting man! He probably owns shares in a brewery. Why, every child knows that teetotalers have the strongest hearts. They learn that before they learn to run.

DEWLIP. Doctors certainly seem very unfamiliar with even the simplest scientific facts. Anyhow, I shall have to go steady: no strain, no excitement, no shocks.

MISS SMITH. It's a shame! I don't think doctors should be allowed. Poor Mr. Dewlip!

DEWLIP. No, you mustn't encourage self-pity! What is it the poet says? "If you can keep your head when all about you Are losing theirs and blaming it on you." Ponder a moment on those very remarkable words, Miss Smith. It is a pity they are not better known. But wait: I have another surprise for you. [*He takes a magazine from his pocket and hands it to her.*]

MISS SMITH. What's this?

DEWLIP. That, Miss Smith, is the house-organ of Dewlip Motors Limited, a monthly journal compiled for and by the firm's employees. On page five you will see my first essay in journalism: an editorial contributed by the Chairman himself.

MISS SMITH. Oh, how lovely!

DEWLIP. I have called it: "That little sunny smile that helps." Do you think that's a good title?

MISS SMITH. [*twinkling with pleasure as she scans the article*] Are you sure it's not a little long?

DEWLIP. I didn't think so. It looks well in print, don't you think?

MISS SMITH. Indeed I do. No wonder you were late.

DEWLIP. Fancy being late, too, to-night of all nights!

MISS SMITH. Any one would think you'd never been to a theater before.

DEWLIP. Nor have I—with you.

MISS SMITH. But even I can't make a good play out of a bad one.

DEWLIP. Can't you? I wonder.

MISS SMITH. [*amiably*] Be careful. No compliments.

DEWLIP. Why would you never come out with me before?

MISS SMITH. I don't think it's right for a young woman to accept hospitality from her employer.

DEWLIP. Yet I am still your employer.

MISS SMITH. You were so persistent. Besides, you had done so many things to please me, it seemed only fair that I should do something to please you.

DEWLIP. [*as who should say "Oh, my dearest!"*] Oh, Miss Smith!

MISS SMITH. It's true.

DEWLIP. Have I really done so much to please you?

MISS SMITH. You have indeed. [*earnestly*] And I'm so terribly, terribly grateful.

DEWLIP. [*fondly again*] Oh, Miss Smith!

MISS SMITH. But listen: there's just one other thing. [*She takes his lapel winningly in her fingers.*]

DEWLIP. [*enchanted*] What is it, Miss Smith?

MISS SMITH. The thing I asked you about this morning: the roulette parties. I know you don't play yourself any-more, but I hate them turning your nice flat into a shambles two or three times a week. I suppose they're coming again to-night? It's Wednesday.

DEWLIP. Would it please you very much if I told you they weren't?

MISS SMITH. *Very* much.

DEWLIP. Well, they aren't. I let them know this morning, after you spoke to me, that there was to be no more gambling here and they must find somewhere else. Just for to-night I asked my mother to let them have a room. She's taken a house off Lowndes Square for the season. There! Are you pleased?

MISS SMITH. [*genuinely delighted*] Oh, Mr. Dewlip!

DEWLIP. Miss Smith!

MISS SMITH. [*breaking at last from their held gaze*] I must go down and change. I shall be late. I'll come up here as soon as I'm ready.

[*At the door she waves gaily. Rapt, he waves back. For a moment he contemplates the door through which she has passed; then goes into his bedroom himself to change.*

After a short silence a bell is heard: then another short silence; then the sound of the flat door being opened, and of voices speaking in the little hall. JULIA *is at last audible.*]

JULIA. [*before she appears*] You needn't announce us. We'll go in and wait.

[*She comes in, followed by her husband. A little grimly she seats herself by the table. Her fingers drum.* JELLIWELL, *clearly in a state of considerable perturbation, paces nervily. The house-organ, lying on the table, catches his eye. He picks it up.*

JELLIWELL. Listen to this. [*reading*] "That little sunny smile that helps," by Henry Dewlip. [*with disgust*] That little sunny smile that helps! Good God!

JULIA. Of course, he's mad! I don't know what's happened to him, but there's no other way of explaining his conduct these last weeks. He's stark, staring mad.

JELLIWELL. It's so difficult to know how to deal with a man in his condition. I simply haven't an idea in my head.

JULIA. You never have.

JELLIWELL. Now don't be offensive, old girl. That won't get us anywhere.

JULIA. I can't help it. I'm sick to death of your dreary helplessness.

JELLIWELL. Well, I don't know that *you're* particularly helpful.

JULIA. Are you supposed to support me, or I you?

JELLIWELL. Well, aren't I supporting you?

JULIA. You are: but being supported on credit doesn't give one a very agreeable sense of security.

JELLIWELL. Now, for pity's sake don't start bullying me about my debts again. I don't know what's happened to us lately: nothing but scrapping. And we used to be such damn good friends.

JULIA. Perhaps we've been seeing too much of each other.

[DEWLIP *comes in. Disturbed in the process of changing, he is coatless, waistcoatless, collarless, and in his stock-inged feet.*]

DEWLIP. Hallo, Johnny. I thought I heard your voice.

JELLIWELL. Hallo, old boy.

DEWLIP. And Julia! How nice to see you, Julia.

JULIA. [*rather unfriendly*] I should like a cocktail.

DEWLIP. There now: what a shame! I haven't a drop of anything in the place.

JULIA. Where's your cocktail cabinet gone?

DEWLIP. Well, the fact is, I sold it. It seemed such a use-less kind of thing to lumber up the place with. One can somehow manage to keep the room much tidier without it. As a matter of fact, it was raffled at a bazaar for the Temperance Society.

JULIA. [*indicating the article on the table*] Did *you* write that?

DEWLIP. [*proudly*] I did.

JULIA. Why?

DEWLIP. Why? What a strange question, Julia dear. Have you read it? What do you think of it?

JULIA. I think your mind's affected. Johnny wants to speak to you.

DEWLIP. Of course, Johnny. What is it?

JELLIWELL. Well, old boy, it's about your letter.

DEWLIP. Yes, I've been expecting to hear from you.

[JULIA *lights a cigarette.*]

JELLIWELL. Well, frankly, I didn't know what to say. It kind of bowled me over. So I thought it was best to come and have a chat about it.

DEWLIP. Very wise, dear friend. There's nothing like a good heart-to-heart talk between man and man.

JULIA. What did you call him?

DEWLIP. Dear friend. Johnny and I, you know, were in the Lower Third together.

JULIA. You must have been very bright boys.

JELLIWELL. Anyhow, to put the thing shortly, you can't do it, old boy, you just can't do it. It's like giving a chap a leg up for the sole purpose of giving him a good kick in the pants and letting him down again. Isn't that so, Julia?

JULIA. I couldn't have put it more elegantly myself.

DEWLIP. My dear Johnny, I am truly grieved that you should look at it like that. But after all, Dewlip Motors is not a philanthropic institution. If my own carburettors are better and cheaper, surely I ought to use them. The fact is, since I've taken a direct hand in the business, I have been lucky enough to introduce a number of small improvements, and this is one of them. The firm, if I may say so without vainglory—

JULIA. Without what?

DEWLIP. Without vainglory, Julia dear. The firm is already beginning to show signs of a general efficiency hitherto unsurpassed in its history. I do not boast. It is just that Providence has seen fit to bless me with a business flair of which, until a few months past, I was completely ignorant.

JELLIWELL. That's all very well, my dear fellow, but what about me? Do you realize it means red ruin for me?

DEWLIP. [still beaming blandly] That's a shame, my friend: it really is. But there! What does the poet say?

JELLIWELL. [impatiently] I don't know, old boy. What does he say?

DEWLIP. He says: "If you can make a heap of all your winnings And risk them on one turn of pitch and toss, And lose, and start again at your beginnings, And never breathe a word about your loss." [*Dressed as he is, there is a touch of incongruity about this declamation.*]

JULIA. [*practically*] Johnny owes just on £4,000. With the Dewlip contract he would have been square inside a year. As it is, the creditors will be down on him as soon as they hear he's lost it. Also, having failed to secure any other contracts, he will have to sell the business. Also, being a congenital greenhorn, he paid too much for it, and he'll have to sell it at a loss.

[DEWLIP *looks from one to the other; then goes to his desk, sits, and writes on a check-form.*]

DEWLIP. I am sorry. I cannot possibly give you back the contract. I am committed too far. But—well—what was the figure you mentioned, Julia?

JULIA. Four thousand pounds.

JELLIWELL. I say, old boy, it's frightfully good of you, but I really didn't mean that.

DEWLIP. Say no more about it, dear friend. We pass through this world but once; therefore, if there is any little good deed or kind action we can do, let us do it now. [*The check is signed and blotted. He hands it to* JELLI-WELL.] There.

JELLIWELL. No, really, old boy. I couldn't dream of accepting it.

JULIA. [*grimly*] Johnny, do you want me to leave you?

JELLIWELL. No, of course, darling, but—

DEWLIP. Julia is right. Accept it for the sake of old times.

JELLIWELL. Very well. But mind, I only accept it in memory of old times.

[*The check changes hands.*]

DEWLIP. That's it. In memory of Stinker, eh?

JELLIWELL. [*with suppressed emotion as he grips* DEW-LIP's *outstretched hand*] In memory of Stinker!

JULIA. Who was she?

DEWLIP. [*with hauteur*] Stinker was Divinity Master of the Lower Third.

JELLIWELL. Good-by, old boy. [*at the door*] Coming, darling?

JULIA. No, I want to speak to Henry. If you go home, I'll join you.

JELLIWELL. Very well, old boy—I mean, darling! [*He goes.*]

DEWLIP. I hate to be inhospitable, my dear Julia, but you've got me at rather an inconvenient moment. I'm a little late already.

JULIA. I won't keep you long. But now that we're alone, please do me the favor of behaving like a human being.

DEWLIP. My dear Julia—

JULIA. Don't make speeches. Just answer my questions. [*crisply*] Number one: do you want to kiss me?

DEWLIP. My dear Julia—

JULIA. The answer is Yes or No.

DEWLIP. No.

JULIA. Good. Number two: why not?

DEWLIP. My dear Julia—

JULIA. Number two: why not?

DEWLIP. I made a mistake in answering number one. To be perfectly truthful, I do want to kiss you. But I'm not going to.

JULIA. Why not?

DEWLIP. I don't think it would be right.

JULIA. Why not?

DEWLIP. Why not! Have you no moral sense at all? Do you think I'm the kind of man to go about the world kissing the wives of my best friend?

JULIA. Yes, I do.

DEWLIP. Well, I'm not.

JULIA. But you were.

DEWLIP. Very likely. I am, however, not the man I was. I have been fortunate enough to see the error of my ways.

JULIA. You'll get such a clout on the ear in a minute.

DEWLIP. I must finish dressing. Is there anything else?

JULIA. [*still very businesslike*] This is the first time for weeks I have been able to see you alone. You have been avoiding me. Question number three: why?

DEWLIP. Because I was not in the least anxious to receive a clout on the ear.

JULIA. You foresaw that that was likely?

DEWLIP. I foresaw that the interview might be delicate.

JULIA. Delicate?

DEWLIP. Disagreeable.

JULIA. Am I to understand, then, that this elaborate buffoonery of yours is no more than the outward manifestations of a reformed rake?

DEWLIP. If you choose to put it like that, yes.

JULIA. Number four: what precisely has reformed you?

DEWLIP. That is a point which at present I have neither the time nor the inclination to discuss. Suffice it that I have my own good reasons.

JULIA. Are you dining with them to-night?

DEWLIP. Since you ask me, I am: to-night.

JULIA. The reformed rake, accompanied by the source of his inspiration, takes to the tiles again: for one night only.

DEWLIP. As a matter of fact, I anticipate an extremely interesting evening. We are going to the Everyman Theater, where they are presenting for the first time in

English, a play from the Jugo-Slav: "Three Sisters in search of a Character."

JULIA. Who is the woman?

DEWLIP. [*loftily*] Woman?

JULIA. Don't be affected. Who is she?

DEWLIP. My secretary: Miss Smith.

JULIA. How perfectly disgusting! You're a danger to the country. A poor little girl who is forced to endure you by the need of money!

DEWLIP. Julia! How dare you!

JULIA. Who probably has an old mother dependent on her, and as like as not a little crippled sister as well! What a subject for your middle-aged persecutions! Lend me your handkerchief. I feel a little sick.

DEWLIP. I shall not lend you a handkerchief. You have insulted me. I overlook it only because you have lost your temper.

JULIA. On the contrary I was never cooler. I shall ask you one more question, then you may go and dress. Number five, I think it is. Am I to understand that you have definitely and finally thrown me over? Answer very carefully, won't you, Henry?

DEWLIP. My dear Julia—

JULIA. [*menacing*] Yes or no, Henry. Am I to understand that that is the case?

DEWLIP. [*defiantly*] Yes. [*Hands behind his back, he strikes an attitude.* JULIA *grits her teeth with rage. She rises.*]

JULIA. [*as soon as she is able to articulate*] Reptile!

[DEWLIP *does not budge. At length infuriated by his superb attitude, she goes to him and stamps her heel vigorously on his stockinged foot; then flounces, chin in air, out of the flat.*]

DEWLIP. [*in agony*] God, you little swine!

[*But there is no sound in response, other than that of a slammed front door. Nursing his foot, he limps back to his bedroom. Presently there is the sound of voices in the hall again, and* JULIA *returns. She looks a little furtively to see that the bedroom door is closed; then takes her handbag from the table where she had left it. For a moment or two she moves about thoughtfully, and is arrested by the sound of an opening door.* MISS SMITH *comes in, just as* JULIA *is making as if to go. They stare at each other for a moment with mutual distrust.*]

MISS SMITH. [*at length*] How do you do?

JULIA. [*sullenly*] How do you do?

MISS SMITH. Are you waiting for Mr. Dewlip? [*a little proprietarily*] I'll call him for you.

JULIA. Please don't trouble. He's changing, and is probably without a shirt. I never think Henry looks his best without a shirt, do you?

MISS SMITH. I haven't had the opportunity of judging.

JULIA. I see: you can't have known him long.

MISS SMITH. I think he won't keep you many minutes now.

JULIA. I'm not waiting for him.

MISS SMITH. Not?

JULIA. No. As a matter of fact, he's just left me.

MISS SMITH. [*smiling with pleasure*] Oh, how rude of him.

JULIA. Not at all. I trod on his toe.

MISS SMITH. That's no excuse for discourtesy. If a man doesn't want a woman's company at any time, he has no right to show it.

JULIA. Oh, Henry and I are such old friends. We don't make compliments. Did I leave the door open? I didn't hear you ring.

MISS SMITH. [*enjoying herself*] No: you see, I have my own latch-key. I'm in and out so much.

JULIA. You're Mr. Dewlip's typist, are you not?

MISS SMITH. [*sweetly*] His secretary, yes.

JULIA. My husband always gets his girls from Baker's. He says they're so hardworking, and *quite* cheap. Were you trained at Baker's?

MISS SMITH. No. But then I probably wouldn't suit your husband. I'm not at all cheap.

JULIA. I understand Mr. Dewlip is taking you to the pictures or something to-night?

MISS SMITH. Yes; to the theater.

JULIA. Dear Henry! He's so good-natured. If he's late, you mustn't be cross with him. It's entirely my fault. Poor fellow, he hadn't seen me for so long. You may tell him you know whose fault it is.

MISS SMITH. But I don't.

JULIA. I am Mrs. Jelliwell. You may have heard Mr. Dewlip speak of me.

MISS SMITH. Oh, of course I have. He and I have discussed you often. [JULIA *stirs uneasily*.] As a matter of fact, the very first letter I ever took from his dictation was to you: a kind of love-letter. I remember being surprised that he should have dictated a letter of that sort. Of course that was before I learnt how lightly Mr. Dewlip took such things. I don't think I ever saw your reply: or indeed, any of the replies. If so, I've forgotten them.

JULIA. [*her foot tapping ominously*] What exactly do you mean by "any of the replies"?

MISS SMITH. Oh, I had to send carbon copies of the letter to two or three other women.

JULIA. [*in a fury*] How dare you speak to me like that!

MISS SMITH. Oh, dear, have I said something indiscreet?

JULIA. I shall report you to Mr. Dewlip for impertinence.

MISS SMITH. I'm sorry, but it never occurred to me that you could have taken Mr. Dewlip seriously. Of course, if I'd guessed for a moment that you were in love with him—

JULIA. I am not in the least in love with him!

MISS SMITH. That's what I thought. After all, you have a husband, haven't you? And I expect he's really very fond of you, even if he does get his girls from Baker's.

JULIA. I have no intention of discussing my affairs with you.

MISS SMITH. Quite right. I think that's very proper and dignified. Still you've no cause really to resent my influence with him. I assure you it's in the right direction.

JULIA. Your influence? I was not aware that you had any.

MISS SMITH. A little, I think. You see, I happen to be rather a believer in the Decent Thing.

JULIA. In what?

MISS SMITH. In decency. [*Instinctively* JULIA, *who is seated, pulls down her skirt an inch or two.*] Mr. Dewlip has come round to my point of view. [*a skeptical snort from* JULIA] For example, it was at my suggestion that he has given up gambling.

JULIA. What!

MISS SMITH. Yes, really. Then I don't think that is the kind of article he would have written three months ago.

JULIA. Well, I'm damned!

MISS SMITH. Again, I believe I'm responsible for his going to work in his own business, and therefore indirectly for his new carburettor designs. But for me the Caribona contract would still hold good.

JULIA. [*rising, appalled*] Do you dare to tell me that you were at the bottom of the Caribona affair?

MISS SMITH. Oh yes!

[JULIA *turns away, exsufflicate with rage.*]

MISS SMITH. And finally, it's really thanks to me that he's given up the company of the many rather worthless women with whom he used to associate.

JULIA. I'll give you worthless women, my girl!

DEWLIP. [*entering*] Ah, Julia: I thought you had gone.

[*He appears, dressed in immaculate tails, a white silk scarf wound about his neck, a silk hat in his hand.*]

JULIA. [*sullenly*] I left my bag here and came back for it.

DEWLIP. [*who is all benevolence*] Ah. I hope you and Miss Smith have managed to entertain each other.

MISS SMITH. Oh, we have. Mrs. Jelliwell I think is really interested in your spiritual welfare.

DEWLIP. Dear Julia.

JULIA. On the contrary: I don't mind if he rots!

DEWLIP. Dear Julia: always such a tease.

JULIA. Henry, I warn you not to annoy me. How's your foot?

DEWLIP. [*limping a few steps towards her*] Oh, not very bad. It should be quite well in a week or two. I'm afraid

I acted on a wicked impulse, Julia: I was wrong to reprove you. I am sorry. After all, you didn't do it on purpose.

JULIA. Rubbish. I did. What's more, if you come within range, I'll do it again.

DEWLIP. I think, my dear Julia, you are perhaps not quite yourself to-night. Furthermore I believe I can guess why.

JULIA. [*rounding on him*] I have no doubt you believe so! [*She launches upon a magnificent, a positively classical crescendo of fury.*] And your girl here believes so! What else should one expect from a pair of minds so concentrated on vulgar, petty intrigue and scullery romanticism? What else should one expect from a complacent buffoon, a dreary, worn-out, used-up, sanctimonious, prematurely aged roué, so consumed with a pitiable, senile vanity as to imagine himself an object of adoration for any woman who allows a charitable impulse to disguise her natural instinct of contempt? In love with you, Henry Dewlip? In love with you, you poor, dim boob? When I fall in love, it's with a man: not with—with "a sunny smile that helps"! [*And with a magnificent sweep, she is gone. But* DEWLIP, *impervious, is still beaming.*]

DEWLIP. How rude!

MISS SMITH. Poor Mr. Dewlip.

DEWLIP. I'm afraid I've kept you waiting. Mrs. Jelliwell delayed me.

MISS SMITH. Never mind. I'm not hungry.

DEWLIP. Aren't you? Nor am I. In any case it's almost too

late for dinner now. Shall we cut it, and have supper after the show instead?

MISS SMITH. All right: that is, if we're hungry.

DEWLIP. [*gravely*] Miss Smith, people can have supper for other reasons than because they're hungry.

MISS SMITH. Can they? Tell me some.

DEWLIP. For example, because they wish to talk. There were certain things I had intended to say to you at dinner to-night.

MISS SMITH. Say them now. We've plenty of time.

[*He considers for a moment: then, his mind made up, sets down his hat on top of the gramophone next to the bowler which he has already left there on his first entrance. In silence, very deliberately, he seats himself, but changing his plans, he moves across and takes post standing with his back to the fire-place.*]

DEWLIP. Miss Smith, a few moments ago we were not alone.

MISS SMITH. That was my impression.

DEWLIP. You will not easily believe me, but the lady who has just left us was until quite recently the object of my very warm regard.

MISS SMITH. Indeed, I can believe you very easily. Personally, I would have put it rather more strongly than that. Have you forgotten the very first letter you ever dictated to me?

DEWLIP. I never sent it.

MISS SMITH. I know, but it represented your feelings at the time. Besides, Mrs. Jelliwell is extremely beautiful. I'm not sure that she's quite the type that I personally admire, but she *is* beautiful.

DEWLIP. She is. But after all, what is beauty? Something quite unimportant. You have taught me that.

MISS SMITH. [*smiling*] That's a little clumsy, isn't it?

DEWLIP. Ah, don't make fun of me You know what I mean. I merely mean that beauty was the only quality in a woman that used to interest me. She could be dishonest, unintelligent, unchaste, deceitful and quarrelsome. Those were faults for her husband to worry about, not me. I sought from women love always, companionship never. In my blindness, in my grossness, I used to say: among men one should look for friends, among women one should look for lovers. And so I had many friends, but not a woman among them; many lovers, but not a friend among them. Superficially it seemed to work well. At my club I was popular to a degree. The bachelors enviously regarded me as their ideal: the married men enviously regarded me as a cad. I was convinced that both were right: and I gloried in it. [*He drops his voice.*] That is to say, until you came along.

MISS SMITH. [*happily*] And then?

DEWLIP. And then; and then for the first time in all these years I learnt what true love was: love of the spirit, pure love. That was it. Pure love for a pure woman. Gosh, it was great! My popularity at the club waned and perished. I became a bore; armchairs emptied magically when I entered. And I was proud of it. Which of those horrid men, I thought, had known a pure love for a pure woman? Not one. Several of them I asked that very question. Good afternoon, So-and-so, I would say, have you ever known a pure love for a pure woman? And So-and-so would look uncomfortable and walk away, so that I could draw but one conclusion: poor So-and-so had not. Probably he had not even known a pure woman. I do not want to make a speech, but in short that, my dear, my very dear Miss Smith, is what you have done for me.

MISS SMITH. [*fondly*] Are you happy; happier for the change?

DEWLIP. Do you doubt it? And you? Are you happy that you have caused the change? [*She nods gently, her eyes tender.*] Miss Smith, I want to ask you something.

MISS SMITH. What is it?

DEWLIP. It's just this. Miss Smith—I say, I can't go through life calling you Miss Smith. What is your Christian name?

MISS SMITH. Why?

DEWLIP. Because I want to use it. May I use it?

MISS SMITH. Perhaps: at least outside office hours. It's Angela.

DEWLIP. [*ecstatically*] Angela!

MISS SMITH. What were you going to ask me?

DEWLIP. What I want to ask you is important. I don't expect an answer immediately, but I can't beat about the
bush. It's just this.

[*The telephone bell rings.*]

MISS SMITH. The telephone.

DEWLIP. [*miles away*] The telephone!

MISS SMITH. The telephone.

DEWLIP. Oh! The telephone! [*He goes to it.*] Hullo. Yes,
speaking. . . . Who? . . . Yes, she is. Hold on. [*to* MISS
SMITH] It's the Hall-porter's wife. She wants to speak
to you.

MISS SMITH. [*taking the receiver from him*] Thank you.
Hallo? . . . Yes. . . . Yes. Asking for me? Is he? . . .
Yes, I *know* he's in bed. I only left him ten minutes ago.
. . . Oh, I *did* kiss him: it's not true. I kissed him again
and again. . . . What? . . . Yes. . . . The darling! . . .
All right. Tell him I'll come in again, but only for a minute. . . . Yes. Thank you so much. [*She replaces the receiver.*] Darling Pierre! He's played this game before.
Why, what's the matter? [*For just then she catches sight
of* MR. DEWLIP's *face. It is discolored with suppressed emotion.*]

DEWLIP. [*grimly*] Who is Pierre?

MISS SMITH. Pierre? Why he's just— You're not ill, **are**
you?

DEWLIP. [*his voice rising*] Who is Pierre?

MISS SMITH. Pierre is my son.

DEWLIP. Your what?

MISS SMITH. My little boy. The Hall-porter's wife looks after him for me. He says I didn't kiss him goodnight.

DEWLIP. Your son? And how in Heaven's name may I ask did *you* come by a son?

MISS SMITH. [*beginning to take umbrage: a little haughtily*] By the usual procedure, Mr. Dewlip.

DEWLIP. Are you completely shameless? You stand there brazenly and—and— Am I to understand—are you going to imply that you—you are married?

MISS SMITH. [*proudly*] Certainly we were married! I think you are a little forgetting yourself.

DEWLIP. [*swallowing his feelings*] Miss Smith, will you kindly hand me my hat. No, I need not trouble you. [*He crosses to the gramophone himself. On his way he stops and lays the theater-tickets on a table in front of her.*] These are the theater-tickets. I shall not require my seat. Do me the favor of asking your husband to make use of it. [*Hat in hand he pauses at the door.*] And if during the intervals you should have an opportunity for meditation, ponder on this thought, Miss Smith: there are more kinds of cheats than one. I wish you good evening.

[*He claps his hat on his head with a dignified gesture that is injured only by the fact that inadvertently he has picked up, not his silk hat, but his bowler. The front door is heard to bang, and* MISS SMITH *is alone.*]

CURTAIN

ACT THREE

ACT THREE

Eleven o'clock next morning. MISS SMITH *is alone, working at her machine. From time to time she halts to listen for somebody's arrival. At length the sound of the front-door bell is followed by the sound of* MR. JELLIWELL'S *voice in the hall.*

JELLIWELL. [*bursting in*] Where's Dewlip? [*He is in a fury.*]

MISS SMITH. Perseus!

JELLIWELL. I'm sorry, my dear. But this is important. Where's your swine of an employer?

MISS SMITH. What do you want him for?

JELLIWELL. I want to wring his neck.

MISS SMITH. Why?

JELLIWELL. Don't ask me now, Andromache. I'm too angry to explain. It's just an impulse. Where is he?

MISS SMITH. Of course I don't want to interfere, but are you quite sure it would be right to wring his neck—you know what I mean—decent?

JELLIWELL. Quite sure. It would be the first decent thing I've done in my life.

MISS SMITH. Not the first, Perseus.

JELLIWELL. Dear child! You have such a soothing effect on a chap. All the same—where is he?

MISS SMITH. I don't know.

JELLIWELL. Oh come, old girl. You're his confidential secretary.

MISS SMITH. Very likely, but he's left me out of his confidence this time.

JELLIWELL. You know he's not at his office, don't you?

MISS SMITH. I do. But how did *you* know?

JELLIWELL. I telephoned. Is he in this flat?

MISS SMITH. No. [*She is standing in front of the bedroom door.*]

JELLIWELL. Andromache, I believe you're shielding him.

MISS SMITH. Nonsense. Why should I?

JELLIWELL. Out of your sweet, generous nature.

MISS SMITH. [*softened*] I assure you I'm not.

JELLIWELL. Then why are you standing slap in front of his bedroom door?

MISS SMITH. Do you think it would be in better taste if I were standing behind it?

JELLIWELL. Andromache, I'm going into that bedroom.

MISS SMITH. [*after contemplating him for a moment*] As you please. [*She moves aside.*]

[JELLIWELL *hesitates, then goes into the bedroom. Soon he comes out again.*]

JELLIWELL. He's not there.

MISS SMITH. Oh, please don't apologize.

JELLIWELL. I'm sorry, old girl: but I had to make sure. I say, do you know, his bed's not been slept in!

MISS SMITH. I know.

JELLIWELL. [*pulled up*] Oh? And *how* do you know?

MISS SMITH. [*sharply*] Perseus! What's the matter with you this morning? How do *you* know it's not been slept in? Did you expect to find it still not made at eleven o'clock in the morning?

JELLIWELL. But it's all turned down; with his pajamas laid out and a black cat fast asleep on the trousers.

MISS SMITH. A black cat?

JELLIWELL. Yes, and, if I'm any judge, liable to have kittens at any moment.

MISS SMITH. Oh, how lucky!

JELLIWELL. It won't be lucky for him if I find him.

MISS SMITH. And where now do you propose to look?

JELLIWELL. I don't know. I've tried his club, and I've tried Vine Street. Can't you help me?

MISS SMITH. All I can tell you is that he left here about half-past seven last night, and hasn't been seen since.

JELLIWELL. Where was he going?

MISS SMITH. He *was* going to the theater, but he changed his mind. I want to find him just as much as you do.

JELLIWELL. *You* want him? Why?

MISS SMITH. They telephoned here for him from his mother's.

JELLIWELL. In the country?

MISS SMITH. No, she's taken a house in town for the season. Poor old lady!

JELLIWELL. Why, what's happened to her?

MISS SMITH. What's happened to her! She's only spent the night in jail.

JELLIWELL. No! What's she done?

MISS SMITH. She's done nothing. It was just bad luck. It appears that the tenant, who had the house just before Mrs. Dewlip, used to use it as a gambling-den, and the police had been watching it. Then as luck would have it, they needs must choose last night to raid it.

JELLIWELL. But suppose they did? Why arrest Mrs. Dewlip?

MISS SMITH. Because she's the present tenant. All Mr. Dewlip's regular roulette gang were playing there.

JELLIWELL. Why there?

MISS SMITH. Mr. Dewlip didn't want them here any more.

He'd had enough; so he sent them to his mother's just for that one night.

JELLIWELL. I don't understand. You mean the police had been watching the place because the previous tenant had used it as a gambling house?

MISS SMITH. Exactly; and when they raided it last night, Mrs. Dewlip was arrested because her son's friends happened to be there playing roulette. Her solicitors are in the country, and she knew nobody here to get her out except Mr. Dewlip. They telephoned for him all over London, but he was nowhere to be found. I think it's a disgrace. If a man can't be at hand when his own mother's arrested, he ought to be ashamed of himself.

JELLIWELL. Dirty dog!

MISS SMITH. Anyway, it's not much use your searching any longer.

JELLIWELL. [stubbornly] Isn't it! I don't give up so easily. What's his mother's address?

MISS SMITH. Thirteen Horseshoe Gardens, Lowndes Square.

JELLIWELL. I shall go there and find out if they've heard anything of him.

MISS SMITH. But why do you want him?

JELLIWELL. [spluttering with indignation] Why do I want him? Can you ask why I want him? He—I—my wife—my own wife!!

MISS SMITH. No!

JELLIWELL. I tell you yes! My own wife! His best friend!

MISS SMITH. And I thought he had changed. Just think of it. That poor creature! Even her! Oh! [*She shudders.*]

JELLIWELL. I tell you nothing is sacred to him.

MISS SMITH. Not even lunacy!

JELLIWELL. What? Oh. No. Quite.

MISS SMITH. Poor, poor Mrs. Brown!

JELLIWELL. Eh?

MISS SMITH. And poor, poor Perseus!

[*She takes his hand and grips it silently in both her own, considerately avoiding his eyes. He returns the pressure; then without another word, his head bowed, his lips manfully compressed, he leaves her. Alone, she ponders a moment, indignantly stamps her foot and returns to her work. Very soon* MR. DEWLIP *returns. He is unshaved: his evening clothes, white silk scarf and bowler hat—which he does not remove—are all soaking wet. She starts and rises quickly at his entrance. He ignores her.*]

MISS SMITH. So you're back!

[*Without even looking at her, he walks to her desk, picks up his letters and begins to read them. Involuntarily he interrupts the perusal of them from time to time by some violent sneezing.*]

MISS SMITH. You've caught a cold.

[*He glances toward her with an expression too negative to be called contemptuous.*]

MISS SMITH. It's been raining.

[*Patiently he opens another letter..*]

MISS SMITH. So you've made up your mind not to speak to me?

DEWLIP. On the contrary, I shall speak to you as soon as I have anything to say.

MISS SMITH. Then why don't you answer me?

DEWLIP. I am not conscious that you have asked me anything. During the last three minutes you have made three very striking observations. First you declared that I was back: then that I had caught a cold: and finally, summoning all your resources for a dramatic climax, you announced defiantly that it has been raining. I agree with you in each respect. I *am* back. [*He sneezes.*] I *have* caught a cold. It *has* been raining. Don't be stupid.

MISS SMITH. You hadn't got a cold last night.

[*He is ostentatiously patient—and silent.*]

MISS SMITH. How did you catch a cold?

DEWLIP. By walking about the Park all night when it was raining.

MISS SMITH. Why did you do that?

DEWLIP. I like the Park. [*She is at a loss for a moment:*

he reads on. Then, still reading, he adds.] You have forgotten to ask me why it was raining.

MISS SMITH. How could you expect any one to find you when you were tucked away in the Park?

DEWLIP. I don't know what you mean by "tucked away," but people *have* been found in the Park. Anyway, I didn't expect to be found.

MISS SMITH. Well, all London's been looking for you. Now you *are* here, you'd better hear the news. Your mother's been arrested.

[*He has just begun another letter and answers absently.*]

DEWLIP. Eh?

MISS SMITH. I said your mother's been arrested.

DEWLIP. [*miles away*] Arrested.

MISS SMITH. Don't you understand me? Arrested. She's spent the night in jail.

[*He finishes the letter and walks across the room taking off his wet coat.*]

DEWLIP. [*almost to himself*] Spent the night in jail. Yes, I know.

MISS SMITH. You know? How do you know?

DEWLIP. [*a touch of anger in his voice*] I called at Horseshoe Gardens this morning, and found out what had happened—thanks to you!

MISS SMITH. Thanks to me? What had I to do with it?

DEWLIP. Oh, don't be so damned innocent! [*He strides up and down, his temper rising.*] Wasn't it thanks to you that they played at my mother's house last night instead of here? Wasn't it thanks to you that I wasn't about when she needed me to bail her out? [*He takes off his hat and throws it viciously into a chair.*] Oh!!

MISS SMITH. [*herself coldly angry by now, her foot tapping*] I'm glad you've at last had the courtesy to remove your hat.

[*For answer he retrieves it and jams it on again, well down to his ears.*]

DEWLIP. [*violently*] There!

MISS SMITH. If you find it a comfort to be childishly rude to me, I'm sure you're very welcome. Perhaps you would like to pull my nose again?

DEWLIP. I would: very much.

MISS SMITH. Isn't it lucky I'm here? A defenseless young woman must be a godsend in such moods as these.

DEWLIP. Defenseless! Why don't you run and tell your— your grotesque husband?

MISS SMITH. Only because I don't happen to have a husband.

DEWLIP. Oho. Now we're coming to the truth. Last night you said you had.

MISS SMITH. That also was the truth. I had.

DEWLIP. But you ceased to have one overnight?

MISS SMITH. On the contrary I ceased to have one over a year ago.

DEWLIP. What happened?

MISS SMITH. I shot him.

DEWLIP. You what?

MISS SMITH. I shot him in the Touraine. [*A long silence.*]

DEWLIP. Rubbish!

MISS SMITH. You don't believe me?

DEWLIP. No.

MISS SMITH. Very well.

DEWLIP. What do you mean by that?

MISS SMITH. I mean it's no good my telling you any more.

DEWLIP. Go on: let's have it all. Suppose I did believe you. You shot him in the Touraine. Why?

MISS SMITH. He was a Frenchman.

DEWLIP. Any other reason?

MISS SMITH. Don't interrupt. He was a Frenchman, and we used to live in the Touraine. I was really very fond of Aristide—

DEWLIP. So you shot him in the Touraine.

MISS SMITH. Do you wish me to tell you or not?

DEWLIP. I'm sorry. Why did you shoot him?

MISS SMITH. I found out after a year that he had a mistress. That I could have put up with, for after all you must expect Frenchmen to be a little bit French. But he began bringing her home to tea. I used to say, "Please, Aristide, dear, don't bring that woman home to tea. Send her some tea, if you like, but it's not right to bring her here for it." He was very sweet to me in his own way and promised he would try not to. But he was rather weak, poor darling, and this was one of the temptations he really couldn't resist. It seemed to him innocent enough. A few months later I found out he had another mistress also; and the climax came when, after fighting against it for some time, he surrendered to an impulse, and invited them *both* to tea. I argued with him very nicely, and pointed out that it would be so bad for little Pierre to grow up thinking that mistresses for tea was in the natural course of things. So I bought a second-hand revolver and said that I was most terribly sorry but, if he did it again, I really would have to take the law into my own hands. Well, poor darling, he did it again. That's all.

DEWLIP. Why weren't you hanged?

MISS SMITH. Hanged? Why should I be hanged?

DEWLIP. It's usual: at least in England.

MISS SMITH. Well, it's not usual in France. The judge was most charming, and the jury were perfectly sweet. They said they wouldn't dream of convicting me. Everybody was extremely sorry for me. The judge declared that in a way I had performed a public service. If husbands began thinking they might bring their mistresses home to tea, he didn't know *what* would happen.

DEWLIP. No doubt the demand for tea would very soon exceed the supply.·

MISS SMITH. [*firmly*] I assure you, to us it was not a laughing matter.

DEWLIP. How long ago was this?

MISS SMITH. About eighteen months. I was twenty-two.

DEWLIP. Wasn't there something in the papers about it?

MISS SMITH. Of course. The papers were full of it.

DEWLIP. What was your husband's full name?

MISS SMITH. Aristide Tantpis.

DEWLIP. So you are Madame Tantpis?

MISS SMITH. I am.

DEWLIP. [*almost to himself*] I remember. So you're the notorious Madame Tantpis! Why do you call yourself Miss Smith?

MISS SMITH. Madame Tantpis is too well-known. Smith is my maiden name. I preferred to work obscurely for my living as plain Miss Smith than to trade on my misfortune as Madame Tantpis. If I had wished, I assure you I could be earning a great deal more than four pounds a week. All the film companies, music-halls and newspapers in the world competed for my services.

DEWLIP. [*reflectively*] Which you offered to me. [*He pauses.*] Miss Smith, I owe you an apology. Last night I was over-hasty. I jumped to conclusions. I should have heard you out. [*He is beaming with pleasure now that she has cleared herself of the charge of matrimony.*] I ask you only to make allowances for me, to consider my state of mind. For weeks you had been the center of all my hopes and plans. I had striven to please you and to please you only. I had trained myself to be what I hoped was a worthy companion for you. And then just as I was on the point of disclosing to you the tenderness that was in my heart, I—[*He sneezes.*]—I discover, as I think, that the prize is unattainable, that your affections are not only engaged elsewhere but engaged legally and irrevocably; and that the contract, moreover, is ratified by no less concrete and palpable a seal than little Pierre. Is it surprising that my equanimity temporarily deserted me? Miss Smith —Angela, was I really so very much to blame?

MISS SMITH. Of course, I understand what you felt, but after all—

DEWLIP. If you understand, that is enough. The old relationship is restored. We can begin from where we left off last night. We can turn over a new leaf. We can—

MISS SMITH. Just one minute.

DEWLIP. What is it, Angela?

MISS SMITH. There's just one further point we may as well clear up.

DEWLIP. What's that?

MISS SMITH. How about Mrs. Brown?

DEWLIP. Mrs. Brown?

MISS SMITH. It will save trouble if you are frank.

DEWLIP. Mrs. Brown?

MISS SMITH. Exactly. Mr. Brown's wife.

DEWLIP. Mrs. Brown?

MISS SMITH. Do you consider the wife of your best friend fair game?

DEWLIP. What are you talking about?

MISS SMITH. Mrs. Brown.

DEWLIP. Who's Mrs. Brown?

MISS SMITH. Please don't pretend. Isn't it rather childish? Isn't it sufficient to have pretended all these weeks that you were a decent-living man with eyes for nobody but me, when all the time you were carrying on a squalid intrique with Mr. Brown's poor mad wife?

DEWLIP. Angela, my dear, I have had a very strenuous night and a most disagreeable morning: I implore you not to complicate my troubles by talking gibberish.

MISS SMITH. The only complication is your lack of frankness.

DEWLIP. Frank! Mrs. Brown! I tell you I don't know any Browns and never have. I know some people called Green and a number of other colors, but Browns, no.

MISS SMITH. Let's drop the subject then, shall we? I see you've determined to be stubborn.

DEWLIP. Perhaps at least you'll have the kindness to tell me where you got hold of this Brown story?

MISS SMITH. Certainly. Mr. Brown called here this morning.

DEWLIP. Oh, did he! Pity I was out. Did he borrow any money?

MISS SMITH. I don't see why you should be spiteful.

DEWLIP. I see. He's not that kind of Brown. Did he leave you in a rage?

MISS SMITH. He arrived in anger, he left more in sorrow. Why do you ask?

DEWLIP. Only because I see some fool's slammed the front door and burst the lock again.

MISS SMITH. You did that when you left last night.

DEWLIP. [*He glances at her resentfully, then deliberately replaces his hat on his head.*] It is being gradually borne in upon me that the chances of our resuming pleasant relations are remote.

[*A short silence falls upon them.*]

MISS SMITH. I'm afraid I haven't been very nice to you since you've come back.

DEWLIP. Not very.

MISS SMITH. I'm sorry. My nerves are upset. There was

your dashing off and leaving me last night without a word; then this Brown business; then not knowing where to find you all the morning. Besides, you must admit you weren't very polite yourself to begin with.

DEWLIP. I wasn't; but I apologized.

MISS SMITH. [*with a very friendly smile*] So do I.

[*She offers her hand. Mollified, he takes it. The door opens suddenly. It is* MRS. JELLIWELL.]

DEWLIP. Hallo, Julia!

JULIA. What are *you* doing?

DEWLIP. Well, as a matter of fact, we were shaking hands.

JULIA. A most original exercise! And that, I presume, is the regulation costume for it.

DEWLIP. [*sneezes*] Julia, please don't quarrel with me; I've got a cold.

JULIA. Has Johnny been here?

DEWLIP. No. Are you expecting him?

JULIA. He'll be here soon. I'll wait. [*She sits.*]

DEWLIP. And in the meantime, what can I do for you?

JULIA. Anything you please except talk to me. Go on shaking hands if you like.

[MISS SMITH, *who has been busying herself with some filing, tosses her head.*]

MISS SMITH. I've finished all the filing. I think I'll go down to my room till you want me. Perhaps you will ring through when you're ready.

[DEWLIP *nods gloomily. She goes. Alone with* JULIA, MR. DEWLIP *looks about him hopelessly for a moment, then seats himself, facing the same direction as she, staring glumly into space. Interminably they sit thus in unbroken silence. Presently he begins to shiver. He gets up, slopes off into the bedroom and returns with an eiderdown under one arm and the black cat under the other. The cat he deposits in the hall. Settling the eiderdown about his shoulders but without removing his hat, he starts the gramophone again and sits miserably beside it. The record that happens already to be in position is "The Death of Asë." His expression unaltered, he resumes his seat. After a long while,* MR. JELLIWELL *comes in.*]

JELLIWELL. [*aggressively*] Oh: so you're back, are you!

DEWLIP. [*gloomily*] Hallo, Johnny.

JELLIWELL. Don't you talk to me!

DEWLIP. [*after blinking a moment with mild incomprehension*] So you're mad too this morning?

JELLIWELL. You'll soon find out whether I'm mad or not.

DEWLIP. [*his gloom unrelieved*] It's very strange: I go away for one night, and the consequence is that, by the time I return, the entire world has lost its balance.

JELLIWELL. [*striding fiercely up and down*] I'll give you balance if you talk to me!

DEWLIP. Therefore I will not talk to you. Julia and I were having a party on the same lines. Sit down and join us. We'll all be mad together.

JELLIWELL. [*stopping the gramophone violently*] I'll tell you what you are: you're vermin, old boy, vermin!

[DEWLIP *doesn't reply, so* JELLIWELL, *a little put out, continues to pace.*]

JULIA. [*to* JOHNNY] Is that all you have to say?

JELLIWELL. Of course not: give us a chance, old girl. I've got this to say: there are some things no decent man will stand for. Heaven knows I'm not narrow-minded. I've knocked up with this one in my time and with—er—that one. I'm a bit of a Bohemian myself. Paris, Vienna, Budapest—I know 'em all. Why, before the War I was three weeks in Port Saïd all alone when—

JULIA. Suppose we skip Port Saïd.

JELLIWELL. Very well, darling. Anyway, Julia will bear me out; no one likes a joke or a bit of wholesome fun more than I do. I don't really even mind—

JULIA. Johnny, it would be so nice if you could come to the point.

JELLIWELL. All right, darling. The point is, for months and months you've been making love to my wife. Now: do you deny it?

DEWLIP. [*without animation*] *Deny it?* Three months ago I attempted to the best of my ability to inform you of it.

JELLIWELL. Three months ago. Exactly. Then Miss Smith came.

DEWLIP. What exactly has she got to do with it?

JELLIWELL. [*turning on him warmly*] Don't you cross-examine me, old boy. Perhaps it may interest you to know that you have wrecked my life—our lives.

DEWLIP. [*not very interested*] Have I, old boy? I hope Julia has been quite truthful with you.

JULIA. Oh, I have been perfectly truthful.

JELLIWELL. Three months ago Julia and I were extremely happy together. She used to see a lot of you, I know, and not very much of me. But when we *were* together, we were damn good pals: weren't we, Julia?

JULIA. We were, Johnny.

JELLIWELL. Then Miss Smith comes. And lo! Julia isn't good enough for my lord. Cools off, he does! Tells her she can go and—and boil herself! He's had enough of her: very sorry, but he doesn't love her any longer. Had enough of her indeed! Had enough of my wife!! Who the Hell do you think you are? After this morning you'll have learnt to treat my wife with some respect. If you think you can throw her away like an old glove or an old sock, you're mistaken! [*He pauses for want of breath.*]

DEWLIP. I see.

JELLIWELL. Oh, you see, do you!

DEWLIP. [*whose despondency throughout has been modi-*

fied only by the mildest interest]. I take it that you have come here this morning to put a formal end, in your own way, to our friendship?

JELLIWELL. Yes, old boy, I have.

DEWLIP. I see. [*He looks from one to the other; then goes to the telephone and removes the receiver.*] Hallo, Mr. Dewlip here. Will you kindly ask Miss Smith to come up.

[*He replaces the receiver.* JULIA *turns quickly.*]

JELLIWELL. What the devil are you going to do?

DEWLIP. [*resuming his seat*] While you have been speaking, I have been thinking. Sit down.

[*Wondering what is coming* JELLIWELL *sits.*]

DEWLIP. So I have wrecked your lives, have I?

JELLIWELL. Yes, you have.

DEWLIP. The happiness you both enjoyed once has left you?

JELLIWELL. It has.

DEWLIP. Moreover, it has left you since I ceased to make love to your wife?

JELLIWELL. Precisely.

DEWLIP. How do you account for that?

JELLIWELL. Why, simply because now we see too much of each other. We get on each other's nerves. That never *used* to happen. It couldn't, when most of the week you used to take her off my hands.

DEWLIP. Johnny always puts things so gracefully.

JELLIWELL. No offense, old girl: but after all, that is the point, isn't it?

[MISS SMITH *comes in.*]

MISS SMITH. [*hesitating*] Oh, I thought you'd be alone. [*Then she notices* JELLIWELL.] Perseus!

JELLIWELL. [*a little discomforted*] Good morning. Er—hallo.

JULIA. [*surprised*] Do you *know* this woman?

JELLIWELL. Er—yes, as a matter of fact, I—er—do. Miss Smith is the lady I—er—met under the omnibus. I think I told you about it. We've—we've run across each other now and again since.

JULIA. [*to* DEWLIP] Did you know anything of this?

DEWLIP. Nothing.

MISS SMITH. Mr. Brown has been extremely kind to me.

JULIA. Mr. Who?

MISS SMITH. Mr. Brown.

DEWLIP. So *that's* Mr. Brown, is it?

MISS SMITH. [*a little taken aback*] *Aren't* you Mr. Brown?

JELLIWELL. Well, not—not altogether.

MISS SMITH. What do you mean by "not altogether"?

DEWLIP. He means he *is* Mr. Brown in places.

JULIA. And when not in those places, he is my husband, John Jelliwell.

MISS SMITH. [*involuntarily*] What? So that is your poor wife. [JULIA *bridles.*] Oh, Perseus, why did you deceive me?

JELLIWELL. My dear, I didn't mean to deceive you. You said you were Miss Smith, and of course I didn't believe you; so I said I was Mr. Brown and never dreamed you believed *me!*

MISS SMITH. [*smiling with relief at so credible an explanation*] How absurd! You silly, my name really is Smith.

JELLIWELL. I'm most frightfully sorry, Andromache. After all, I'd nothing to conceal. You do believe me, don't you? [*She nods.*] Am I forgiven?

MISS SMITH. Of course you are.

JULIA. Touching little scene!

DEWLIP. The scene being concluded, I propose to take the stage. Miss Smith, perhaps you will sit down. [*She does so.*] Johnny, kindly be seated. [*With an inquiring eye on* DEWLIP, *he sits.*] Julia?

JULIA. I prefer to stand.

DEWLIP. That would be a serious mistake.

JULIA. And why?

DEWLIP. Because I am about to make an exceedingly long speech. [*And so she consents. Very deliberately he takes up position in front of them, seated as they are in a row, and, in his own time, begins.*] Ladies and gentleman, what I have to say is, I am afraid, largely autobiographical. I want you to call to mind for a moment the person who was Henry Dewlip three short months ago. I idled away my day and rioted away my night. My temper was short, I gambled and drank to excess, and the truth was not in me. I made love so promiscuously, so ubiquitously and, I may say, so successfully that I was a danger to the community. And no one did I pursue more strenuously than the wife of my best friend, Julia Jelliwell. I was, in short, an unconscionable blackguard. But what happened? Miss Smith happened. I will not conceal it from you: with Miss Smith I fell in love.

MISS SMITH. Oh, please.

DEWLIP. Allow me. In a sense it was for the first time. I had never loved quite in that fashion before. I realize now that all I had felt previously was a simple, unhallowed animal desire. [*He raises his hat politely in the direction of* JULIA.] This was the first time that I had experienced what is known as a pure love: a pure love for a pure woman. What was the result? I gave up drink, I gambled no more, my temper improved, I worked like a slave, I acquired some ideals, I banished every ignoble thought of women from my mind. Julia adored me—

JULIA. Liar! Liar!

DEWLIP. But I was firm. She had to go. But were these the only results? Oh, no, there were others. I developed a weak heart; I became an outcast at my own club; the excellent business prospects of the man who was with me through the War and the Lower Third were destroyed at a blow; it cost me no less than four thousand golden sovereigns merely to postpone his bankruptcy; my mother spent a night in jail; Julia called me a reptile and trod on my toes; I lost all my friends; I ruined my evening clothes and caught a cold; I wrecked the hitherto happy lives of Johnny Jelliwell, who was my best friend, and of Julia Jelliwell, who has the best figure in London. But was it not worth it? It was all for love. Was it not a hundred times worth it? No, by Heavens, it was not! [MISS SMITH *rises, as if she had been pricked.* JULIA's *eyes open wide with pleased surprise.*] The world well lost for love! What craven, abject, pettifogging cur invented that most disgusting phrase? Some men are wolves and some are sheep, but nothing is more deplorable than the one masquerading as the other. Julia: will you kindly come here.

[*Very amiably,* JULIA *comes.*]

JULIA. What is it, Henry?

DEWLIP. [*setting his arm defiantly about her shoulders*] Yesterday, I told you, Julia, that in my opinion it would be wrong to kiss you.

JULIA. You did, Henry.

DEWLIP. To-day, I have changed that opinion. It would be wrong not to. I am told on good authority that Ibsen said, "Be yourself." I have decided to do what Ibsen said. [*He kisses her.* MISS SMITH *turns her back and, betrayed only by a tapping foot, stares ostentatiously through the window.*]

JELLIWELL. [*only just able to express his delight*] I say, old boy, this is splendid. Am I to understand that you're in love with Julia again?

DEWLIP. Love? I would not sully our relations with that tawdry word! I *want* her; simply and honestly, as primitive man wanted his mate, as any decent, self-respecting animal to-day wants his fellow-animal, as the eagle wants his fellow eagle, as the cow wants his fellow cow. Do I want her because I love her? Is this a pure love for a pure woman? Not it: not she. I want her because she has the best figure in London. Divorce her, if you like. Indeed, I wish it. You may even cite me as your co-respondent. It would do me good. I am so revolted with my last three months that nothing, I believe, will take away the unclean taste from my mouth until I have been through the relatively wholesome mud of the divorce courts.

JELLIWELL. [*enthusiastically wringing the hand that is not engaged on* JULIA'S *shoulder*] My dear Henry, I withdraw all I said.

DEWLIP. My dear Johnny, it is already forgotten. As for you, Miss Smith, I can only regret the pain all this must be causing you. You had, I know, expected to marry me. [MISS SMITH *turns with an indignant protest on her lips: but he cuts in at once.*] No, you need not say anything. Please do not blame yourself. I accept full responsibility But we may as well be frank. During these last weeks you had learnt to reciprocate the affection I honestly imagined I felt for you. It is a pity, but that, my dear Miss Smith, is Life.

MISS SMITH. [*icily*] Will you kindly allow me to speak for a moment now? It is true I have been forced to be present at several rather odious and embarrassing "love-scenes," but in your self-preoccupation you no doubt omitted to observe that in each of them *I* played the rôle of resigned and slightly disgusted spectator. I was brought up to listen politely. It seems I was brought up just a little too well. As to marrying you, I assure you my mind has never even been crossed by that extremely obscene idea. Indeed, it was agreed very many weeks ago that, if ever he should be free again, I would marry Mr. Jelliwell.

JULIA. What!

DEWLIP. The devil it was!

JULIA. Johnny, is that true?

JELLIWELL. Well, old girl, it is more or less true.

DEWLIP. Well, I'm damned! And Johnny a married man! What became of your principles all of a sudden?

MISS SMITH. If it weren't for our unjust divorce laws, Johnny wouldn't *be* a married man.

DEWLIP. Unjust?

MISS SMITH. Do you consider it just that a man should be tied up all his life to a woman who's out of her mind?

JULIA. God, let me get at her! [*But* DEWLIP *holds her back.*]

DEWLIP. Julia, I entreat you, keep calm. Johnny, the lady appears to know a great deal about your private life: are you sure you know as much about hers? Did you know, for example, that she had a husband already?

JELLIWELL. A what?

DEWLIP. Husband, husband, husband.

JELLIWELL. Andromache!

DEWLIP. Oh, she hasn't got him any more. She shot him in the Touraine.

JELLIWELL. Don't be absurd, old boy. If she shot him, how could she be here now?

DEWLIP. You're allowed to in France. They have different rules.

JELLIWELL. [*dazed*] But why? Why should she?

DEWLIP. When they were married, they had mistresses for tea. There was therefore no alternative. It was the Decent Thing.

JELLIWELL. Andromache, darling, you hear what he's saying! He says you're a murderess, old girl! Is it true?

MISS SMITH. Quite true.

JELLIWELL. But, darling, why didn't you tell me?

MISS SMITH. I would have told you but you never asked me. After all, it's hardly the kind of thing one chatters about socially. [*winningly*] Does it make any difference? Do you mind?

JELLIWELL. Of course I don't mind, old girl. You shoot what you like. But I would like to have been told.

DEWLIP. Perhaps she'll promise to tell you next time. [*But* JELLIWELL *and* MISS SMITH *are already gone. He looks at* JULIA *for a second and she at him. His toe taps complacently. And then he starts the gramophone. He is still absorbed in this favorite diversion when* JULIA, *lightly whistling the tune of the record, gets up and strolls aimlessly about the room. At first he doesn't notice that she has left his side but, when he does, he looks up and finds her hovering near the bedroom door—hovering and finally passing through it. For a second or two he is alone and then, girding his eiderdown about him, he proceeds to follow her. En route, however, he notices the battered hat still in his hand.*] Oh, I don't need that. [*He puts it down carefully and continues on his way, closing the door behind him.*]

CURTAIN

OTHER TITLES AVAILABLE FROM SAMUEL FRENCH

THE RAPE OF THE BELT
Benn W. Levy

Comedy / 3m, 7f / Exterior
For his ninth labor, Heracles is required to wrest from the queen
of the Amazons her belt. Zeus and Hera comment wittily on the
events.

"The characters are witty and... the story is frothy and
politely risque"
– *New York Journal American*